"That Was Crazy," She Gasped As Soon As He Ended The Kiss.

"Not crazy," he corrected, "wonderful." Keaton framed her face with his fingers and held her still so he could look into her eyes. "If you cook like you kiss, I'm going to be in trouble."

"In trouble how?"

"I won't be able to stop myself from wanting more."

Color flooded her cheeks. Lark hooked her fingers around his hands and pulled them away from her face. "I don't think you'll have to worry on either account."

"What makes you say that?"

"Because you've never struck me as a man who does anything that isn't good for him."

"What about kissing you isn't good for me?"

She set her hands on her hips and regarded him incredulously. "Have you forgotten the bad blood between our families? It already forced Skye and Jake out of town. Can you imagine how bad it would be if we were caught?"

"So what are we supposed to do with these feelings between us?"

"What feelings? It just a simple case of proximity lust. Nothing more."

Keaton studied her, wondering if that was what she truly believed, or if it was a way to let him off the hook. "Is *proximity lust* a scientific term, or something you just made up?"

Because of
the Baby...
CAT SCHIELD

First published in Great Britain 2015
by Mills & Boon, an imprint of Harlequin (UK) Limited,
Large Print edition 2015
Eton House, 18-24 Paradise Road,
Richmond, Surrey, TW9 1SR

© 2015 Harlequin Books S.A.

Special thanks and acknowledgment are given to
Cat Schield for her contribution to the
Texas Cattleman's Club: After the Storm miniseries.

ISBN: 978-0-263-25984-1

CAT SCHIELD

has been reading and writing romance since high school. Although she graduated from college with a BA in business, her idea of a perfect career was writing books for Mills & Boon®. And now, after winning the Romance Writers of America 2010 Golden Heart Award for series contemporary romance, that dream has come true. Cat lives in Minnesota with her daughter, Emily, and their Burmese cat. When she's not writing sexy, romantic stories for Mills & Boon® Desire, she can be found sailing with friends on the St. Croix River, or in more exotic locales, like the Caribbean and Europe. She loves to hear from readers. Find her at www.catschield.com. Follow her on Twitter, @catschield

To Sunshine Grandahl
for sharing her preemie experiences,
and Sarah M. Anderson for being
such a fantastic collaborator.

One

Lark Taylor gathered a deep breath as the elevator doors opened. Plastering a pleasant expression on her face, she straightened her spine. Time to go to work. With a cake box balanced carefully in her hands, she strode down the short hallway to the nurses' station in front of the ICU. The three women behind the desk didn't notice her approach, or if they did, they ignored her.

"So I told him if he thinks he's going hunting two weekends in a row, he can find a new girlfriend." Marsha Todd, a forty-year-old divorced woman with no kids, was holding court as usual. With her bleached teeth, flawless makeup and manicured nails, she was the same sort of shallow individual who had tormented Lark in high school. "So naturally he's staying home. He might not be the brightest guy I've dated, but he's smart enough not to mess with all this."

Jessa and Chelsea, the two other nurses working the ICU today, laughed in appreciation. Taken separately, either woman was tolerable to work with. Jessa was a quiet single mom with a three-year-old son and Chelsea had an alcoholic husband who worked construction. With Marsha as their ringleader, however, they took on a pack mentality. Which meant, if they didn't want to be on the bottom of the pecking order, they'd better make sure someone else was. That person was Lark.

"You're early," Marsha remarked, her tone pitched in criticism as Lark set the cake box on the counter.

"I'm going to spend some time with Grace. I just wanted to drop this off first."

"What is it?" Jessa asked. The nicest of the trio, she had borne the brunt of Marsha's bullying until Lark transferred to the ICU three months ago.

"A cake for Marsha's birthday tomorrow."

"You bought me a cake?"

"Actually I made it."

Chelsea opened the cake box and peered in. "You made this? Really? Looks store bought."

"It's a hobby of mine."

"It's beautiful." Jessa's brown eyes were wide with appreciation. "How long did this take?"

"A couple hours," Lark said, her anxiety easing beneath her coworkers' admiration.

"How did you do the flowers?" Jessa asked. "The roses look real."

"I use a frosting tip and something called a rose nail."

Marsha barely glanced at the three-layer white cake painstakingly decorated in a basket weave pattern with buttercream frosting and royal icing daisies, roses and forget-me-nots. "If it's not gluten free, I can't eat it."

"Sorry, I didn't know that."

"I don't know how. I talk about it all the time." But never to Lark.

"I guess I'm so focused on the patients." Lark realized even as she uttered the excuse that it was the wrong thing to say. "I haven't heard you mention it."

"And speaking of patients," Marsha said, shooting looks at both Jessa and Chelsea. "We'd better get in and check on them."

All three of her coworkers walked away, abandoning Lark at the desk with her cake and her disappointment. Her efforts to make friends with the other nurses these last few months had all been a bust. Marsha was top of the social order in the ICU and she didn't like Lark.

Not knowing what to do with the birthday cake that Marsha couldn't eat, Lark took it down to the surgical floor. She knew her former coworkers would appreciate the treat. Leaving the cake box on the desk of her friend Julie with a brief note explaining what had happened, Lark headed to the stairs.

One floor down from the surgery floor was the maternity ward. Lark had worked at the hospital for three years without ever setting foot on the floor where children were born until a fateful night three months ago when her niece was born. Estranged from her sister these last four years Lark hadn't been able to tell the medical staff when Skye was due, but they'd been able to surmise she was about twenty-eight or twenty-nine weeks along.

Reaching the third-floor landing, Lark headed to the door that would take her into the maternity ward. She put her hand on the door and pushed it open an inch, finding her way blocked by a broad shoulder clad in a navy blue cotton shirt. Dark brown hair in desperate need of a cut curled upward against the shirt's collar.

The tall, ruggedly built man on the other side of the door was Keaton Holt, brother of the man Lark's sister had run off. She seldom encountered him around Royal. He spent most of his time at the family ranch and only made occasional visits into town. She usually heard about those from her father, who complained every time Keaton showed up at the Texas Cattleman's Club.

All that had changed after the tornado ripped through town and a pregnant Skye had been discovered in her overturned rental car.

Keaton was talking on his cell, fully engaged in conversation, and hadn't noticed her presence. Lark would have to interrupt in order to get past. It would mean she'd catch Keaton's attention and have to brave the intensity of his sharp blue gaze that seemed to see straight through her.

As Lark debated retreating back down the stairs and avoiding Keaton altogether, his words floated through the narrow crack between the door and frame.

"That's why I demanded we get the DNA test run. You're Grace's grandmother. You shouldn't be limited to staring at her through the NICU window."

"Of course Grace is his daughter. He and Skye were madly in love when they left Royal." Keaton's voice rang with arrogant confidence that chafed Lark's already frayed nerves. "He chose her over his family. And yeah, he's a stubborn jerk, but if things had ended between them, we'd know."

Lark leaned as far forward as she dared, her curiosity getting the better of her. Day after day she'd sat beside her sister's unconscious body, desperate to know what Skye had been doing in the years since she left town. Did Keaton have the answers?

"I don't know where Jake is." And Keaton sounded far from happy about that. For the last few months, Lark had rebelled against the possibility that Jake was Grace's father. He'd made no attempt to get in contact with Skye in the three months since she was hurt by the tornado that had devastated Royal. That was why Lark had resisted the DNA test as long as she had. What sort of man abandons his child and the woman he loves? A no-good Holt, that's who.

"I haven't been able to get a hold of him. I've called his company several times, but his assistant has given me the runaround. From some of his other staff I was able to find out that he's out of the country, but they refused to give me any more information, so I have no idea where he's gone."

Until this moment Lark hadn't realized that Jake didn't know about Skye. She'd just assumed that he hadn't rushed to Skye's side because their relationship was over. Skye wore neither an engagement nor a wedding ring, and her fingers hadn't borne any telltale band of paleness that indicated a ring had recently been removed. Given how passionate their love had been when they first left Royal, Lark couldn't believe Jake and Skye had been together four years without making some legal commitment to each other. Especially after Skye became pregnant.

"Of course I explained that Skye was hurt. His assistant…" Keaton's frustration was audible, but there was pain in his voice, as well. After a long moment, he continued. "The last time I called for Jake, she told me that she'd been informed he didn't have a brother."

Despite the animosity that existed between their families, Lark winced in sympathy. She and Skye hadn't had any contact these last four years either. She'd been shocked upon moving back to Royal to discover Skye and Jake were still involved and actively hiding their relationship from their parents. Several times in the few months between Lark's return to Royal and Skye's departure with Jake, Lark had warned her sister that she was making a huge mistake trusting a Holt. When Skye chose Jake over her family, Lark had said some harsh things.

She'd accused Skye of being selfish and inconsiderate. At the time Lark had believed her indignation was righteous, but as the years passed, she realized that what she'd perceived as concern for her parents was really resentment born of envy that her sister had chosen to be happy.

"It's okay, Mom. I get that Jake hasn't been able to forgive me for putting them in a position where they felt they had no choice but to leave town," Keaton said, his tone dark. "I can live with being disowned by him. But that doesn't mean I stopped caring about him or his family. He and Skye might not be married, but she is still family. That's why I wanted proof that Grace is his daughter."

"Excuse me." Someone had asked Keaton to step aside.

He nodded and moved out of the way before continuing. "The DNA test should be back today or tomorrow. In the meantime I hired an investigator to find out where Jake has gone."

Before Lark could move, the door she'd been leaning against was pulled away. Off balance, she stumbled into the hallway that led to the NICU. After she made a couple ungainly sidesteps, someone caught her by the arm, steadying her.

She glanced up at her savior. Softened by a thick fringe of black lashes, Keaton Holt's denim-blue eyes captured her full attention. At five feet ten inches, Lark rarely encountered a man she could look up at. Keaton towered over her, making her feel normal. Maybe even a little dainty.

The heat at her center had worked its way into her cheeks by the time she realized she wasn't standing on her own two feet, but still relying on his support. She should have regained her balance and gotten the heck out of there. Keaton and Gloria had to be wondering if she'd been listening in on their conversation. But the leashed strength of the man slammed into her like a runaway calf.

Gripped by what could only be described as a rush of lust, Lark floundered in confusion. Starting when she was a baby, her father's bedtime stories had revolved around the wrongs inflicted on her family by the Holts. She couldn't possibly want Keaton Holt.

"Thank you." She disengaged her arm and took an awkward step back. With effort she ripped her attention away from his sculpted lips. Twenty feet away the room that housed the smallest and sickest babies offered refuge. "Excuse me."

"Lark." Keaton's deep voice rumbled through her as she fled. "Lark, we need to talk."

His voice didn't recede the way it should if she was escaping him. Bracing herself, Lark stopped beside the door that led into the NICU unit.

"The DNA results are due shortly."

"I know," she mumbled, miserable at the idea that she'd have to share Grace with any of the Holts. Unfortunately and against her better judgment, she was also sympathetic to their plight. If she'd been denied access to her niece, she would be beyond miserable.

"We need to talk about what's going to happen next."

"Nothing is going to happen."

"That's not really the case, is it? Once the test determines that Grace is Jake's daughter then I have the same obligation to her as you do."

"Obligation?" Did he seriously think what she felt for Skye and Grace was born of responsibility? She loved her sister and would do everything in her power to take care of Grace. "You think it's your duty to step up because your brother is nowhere to be found." Lark's earlier compassion was trampled beneath an onslaught of annoyance. "You needn't bother. I have matters well in hand."

"I don't think of it as a duty, but I do feel responsible because Jake isn't here."

"And why isn't he?"

"I'm pretty sure he doesn't know what's going on." Keaton set his hand on his hip and gazed beyond her shoulder. "If he did, he'd be at her side."

Lark wasn't at all convinced. "What makes you think they're even still together?"

"My brother loves Skye. Grace is his daughter."

Keaton's thick brows drew together. "That's all the proof I need."

Having had no way to reach her sister these last four years, Lark understood his frustration, but she wouldn't give him the satisfaction of admitting it. "Did you let him know Skye was hurt?"

Keaton's expression shifted into stoic lines. "I've spoken with his assistant, but she's refusing to forward any messages."

"That's quite an excuse." Lark blew out a breath. "If he and Skye were still together I believe he'd have moved heaven and earth to be here for her and Grace. I don't think he's her father."

But she wasn't as convinced as she pretended to be. Grace had Holt eyes and bone structure. That was why Lark had resisted the DNA test for so long. Her instincts told her Grace was Jake's daughter, but the feud that existed between the Taylors and Holts made it so hard for Lark to do the right thing. In the end Keaton's determination and threats of legal action had worn her down.

"Then who is Grace's father and where is he?" Keaton demanded.

Lark had no more idea what had been going on between Skye and Jake than Keaton did, and she wasn't going to pretend any different. "I don't have a clue. We haven't spoken since she left Royal."

Seeing Keaton's surprise, Lark continued. "I didn't think running away with your brother was a good idea and told her so."

"Because you didn't think a Holt was good enough for her?" Keaton's neutral tone kept his comment from sounding bitter.

Lark didn't want to fight with Keaton. She was sick of their families being at war. "I knew my father would disown her if she left."

Skye had always been her parents' favorite. They understood her. Unlike Lark, she'd been pretty and popular in school. She didn't lock herself away in books. Their parents didn't care that Skye's grades were good enough to keep her in the top twenty-five percent of her class; they loved the fact that she was a cheerleader and voted prom queen her senior year.

"I guess we have more in common than either of us knew."

"Seems we do." Tightness eased in Lark's chest. Regret had been her constant companion for four years. It had been a lonely time. Her parents refused to talk about Skye, and Lark had been too ashamed at how she'd treated her sister to confide in any of her friends.

"Thank you for letting me do the test." Keaton's voice softened. "My mother desperately wants to visit her granddaughter."

Regret swamped her at his words. Lark wished her parents had similar desires. "My parents haven't seen Grace." The words spilled out of her with more bitterness than she'd intended.

"But once she leaves the hospital, they can see her as much as they want." Keaton had misinterpreted Lark's meaning.

"The problem is they don't want to see her."

Despite the harm that had befallen their daughter, Tyrone and Vera Taylor hadn't set aside their resentment over Skye's choosing to run off with a hated Holt. Oh, they'd visited her in the beginning when she was first brought in and they acted genuinely concerned, but as the months passed and Skye didn't wake after the medical treatment that induced her coma ceased, they'd retreated into bitterness.

"I don't understand."

"They still can't forgive Skye for running off with your brother."

"Don't you think this thing between our families has gone on too long?"

"Maybe." Everything she'd ever been told by her parents made her want to keep Keaton and his family as far from Grace and Skye as possible, but deep in her heart she knew that if Keaton was right and Jake was Grace's father, the Holts deserved equal time with her. "But you can't expect decades of mistrust to evaporate overnight."

"Jake and Skye got the ball rolling. The rest of us have had four years to adjust."

His challenge settled a huge weight on her shoulders. She was supposed to mistrust him, dislike him even. Since the late 1800s their families had been fighting over the ownership of two thousand acres dotted with several lakes, owned by Lark's family, that bordered the Holts' ranch. She'd grown up listening to her grandfather and father rant about what liars and cheats the Holts were. Never to be trusted. How they were willing to do whatever it took to take what didn't belong to them.

Lark was sick of the feud. It had started with a bill of sale that had gone missing back in 1898. Edwin Holt claimed Titus McMann had sold him the two thousand acres in order to fund his trip to Alaska where gold had been drawing prospectors since the 1880s.

Unfortunately, Titus had died before he could leave town and when Holt's bill of sale couldn't be found in the town records, his brother subsequently sold the land to John Taylor. Although there was nothing overtly suspicious about Titus's death, the fact that both the money he'd received from Edwin Holt and the bill of sale had mysteriously disappeared caused Holt to insinuate John Taylor had been up to no good.

A hard headed, unforgiving man, John Taylor hadn't appreciated the trouble Holt's allegations caused his family and did everything in his power to ruin his neighbor's business and reputation.

Lark hated that her parents continued to be obsessed with the ancient land dispute. They couldn't just let it go. It would be one thing if they'd been the ones who'd lost the land, but they'd won and couldn't rise above their hostility. And she was ashamed that she'd let their spiteful rhetoric poison her against her own sister, something she'd give anything to fix. If only Skye would wake up.

"I heard they're going to release Grace in the next few days," he continued.

"I know." The news that her niece was healthy enough to leave the hospital brought with it both excitement and panic.

"Are you planning on taking her home?"

Something about the intensity in Keaton's manner warned Lark that this wasn't just an innocent question. "Yes."

"She's just as much my responsibility as yours."

"You don't know that. If you did, you wouldn't have asked for a DNA test to prove she's your brother's daughter."

"The test isn't for me," Keaton assured her. "I trust that Jake and Skye are together and want everyone else to know it too."

"What makes you so sure?" Lark asked, wanting him to reassure her.

"Your sister loves my brother. She'd never leave him."

Then why had Skye been returning to Royal and where was Jake?

"I have to start work in forty-five minutes," Lark said. "I really want to go spend some time with Grace before that happens."

"What are your plans for her care while you're working?" Keaton's blunt question caught her unprepared.

Lark usually worked four twelve-hour shifts in a row and then had six days off. She liked the schedule, but it was going to make being Grace's primary caretaker a little challenging. Lark had no intention of putting the tiny baby in day care and she didn't like the idea of a stranger watching her while Lark was at work. She'd hoped her mother might be willing to watch her grandchild, but thanks to Skye's estrangement from the Taylor family, Lark was pretty sure the answer would be no.

"I haven't finalized anything."

"Good."

"Why good?"

"Because I intend to be involved."

Keaton saw immediately that Lark didn't like what he had to say.

"Involved how?"

"I'm going to take care of her while you're working."

"You, personally?" She shook her head. "What do you know about babies?"

"What I don't know I can learn."

"Don't you have enough going on with rebuilding your ranch?"

When the tornado had torn through in October, the Holt ranch house had been demolished along with several of the outbuildings. Fortunately Keaton's parents had been out of town and most of the ranch hands had been miles away checking the fence line for breaks.

Keaton and a few of his employees hadn't been so lucky. Most of the men working nearby had made it to shelter before the tornado hit, but Keaton and his foreman had been in the barn. Jeb had suffered a minor concussion and Keaton's shoulder had been dislocated by flying debris.

Because of the number of people injured by the tornado, Lark had been working in the ER when

Keaton drove himself and three other injured men to the hospital. He recalled the way his spirits had lifted at the briefest flash of awareness that had sparked between them as her eyes first met his. A second later she'd blinked and became all business as she sorted out the extent of their injuries.

The fleeting connection reminded him of simpler days when they'd been kids and he found her both appealing and a curiosity. The three-year difference in their ages and the feud between their families had given him plenty of reasons to give her a wide berth. But it hadn't stopped him from wondering about her.

"My foreman can supervise when I'm not there and call me if something needs my immediate attention." He was determined to protect his brother's paternal rights. "I'm not negotiating with you, Lark."

A mulish expression settled over her features. "Do you even have a place you can care for her? Where are you living while your ranch house is being rebuilt?"

"A hunting cabin."

"A cabin?" Lark crossed her arms over her chest. "I don't think so. A preemie's lungs are delicate. She needs to be in a clean, warm environment free from drafts and damp."

"My parents are staying with friends in Pine Val-

ley. I could bring her there on the days you work."
He made the suggestion knowing it would never fly.

"That would be a terrible imposition on your parents' friends."

"Then I'll watch her at your house."

Lark's eyes widened. Her mouth popped open, but she must have recognized the determination on his face, because whatever refusal she'd been about to utter didn't come. Her facial muscles shifted into unhappy lines.

"I don't really think…" she began before turning toward the door to the NICU. "Do you have any idea what it's like to take care of a baby?"

"Some."

Giving him a doubtful frown, Lark motioned for him to follow her. Her stiff posture demonstrated she wasn't happy with his determination to be involved with Grace. Too bad. As her uncle, he had as much right to be with the infant as Lark.

In silence they walked down the row of incubators to the crib that held Grace. The anxious burn in Keaton's chest whenever he visited his niece had faded. Born ten weeks premature at two pounds, two ounces, the baby girl had gained almost three pounds since then and was now free of all sensors, IVs, pressurized oxygen and the feeding tube.

Acting as if Keaton had ceased to exist for her,

Lark carefully picked up Grace and settled her into the crook of her left arm. "Hello, beautiful. How are you doing today?"

"She's doing great," said Ginger. The nurse on duty was a plump woman in her midforties with keen brown eyes and an engaging smile. "Ready to go home in a few days."

"I'm really excited about that," Lark said, adjusting Grace's pink hat embroidered with the word *Miracle*.

"Are you ready?"

"I have tomorrow off. I'm going to go shopping for everything."

"We're going shopping," Keaton corrected her, drawing Ginger's gaze. "Grace is my niece, as well. I'm going to be involved with taking care of her."

Ginger's eyes brightened. "That's wonderful. Grace is going to need a lot more care than the average baby. I'm glad you're going to be helping Lark out." The NICU nurse gave his arm a pat as she moved off to check on another infant.

"It's premature to talk about your involvement," Lark muttered as soon as the other nurse was out of earshot. "Grace's paternity has not yet been determined."

"Today or tomorrow we'll have the results and you'll see she's my niece as much as yours." Seeing the way Lark's mouth tightened, Keaton continued. "I intend to share the responsibility."

"A lot of men wouldn't want the responsibility of a preemie."

"I know Jake would expect me to take care of his daughter."

He wasn't surprised when she didn't respond. Lark had always struck him as the ultimate wallflower. Quiet and reserved, she watched more than participated. Why had he noticed her at all? Probably because he had similar tendencies. He kept to himself, enjoying the solitude of his cabin beside the small five-acre lake after a hectic day spent managing the ranch.

Her preoccupation with the baby gave him a chance to study her at length. Dressed in pale green scrubs, her wavy blond hair cut in a short bob, she gave off an *ignore me* vibe. She might have gone unnoticed if she wasn't so tall. At five feet ten inches, she would have made a great basketball or volleyball player, but she'd been more of a bookworm than an athlete. She and Jake had been classmates, but despite the fact that he'd been secretly dating her sister all through high school, Lark had never been part of the same crowd.

Three years older than Lark, the single year they'd attended the same in high school, Keaton hadn't had any contact with her, but she'd been extremely intelligent and that intrigued him. With a perfect score on her ACTs and could have had her pick of colleges if she'd wanted to venture out of Texas.

"Can you hold Grace for a second?"

Keaton blinked himself out of his thoughts. "Excuse me?"

"Can you hold Grace?"

"Why?"

Lark's long lashes fluttered upward as she glanced at him in confusion. "Because she needs to be changed and I need to go get some wipes. This is out." She pointed to a box on a nearby shelf.

Keaton stared down at Grace with his hands at his sides. She was so tiny. And he was a big guy more accustomed to wrestling with querulous calves than handling fragile things like a five-pound baby.

Lark stood and held Grace out to him with an impatient "here."

Alarm flashed through him. Keaton took an involuntary step backward. Still staring at Grace's precious face with its soft, perfect skin, he clasped his hands behind his back, feeling the rough scrape of calluses. It wouldn't be right to touch her delicate skin with anything so abrasive.

"Keaton?" Lark's tone had softened. "What's wrong?"

"She's really small." He paused. "And…"

"You're afraid to hold her."

"No."

"How do you expect to help me take care of her when you aren't comfortable enough to hold her?"

He let a breath hiss out from between his clenched teeth before replying, "I'm going to be fine. I just need a little time to get used to her."

"No time like the present." Lark moved into his space, her manner determined. "Give me your left arm."

He resisted her imperious tone for only as long as it took her to lift her gaze to his. She had the greenest eyes, like spring grass after a week of rain. How had he never noticed how beautiful they were? She raised her eyebrows at him. Moving slowly, giving her plenty of time to change her mind, Keaton let his arm swing forward.

She took ahold of his wrist and placed his arm against his abdomen. Her fingers were warm and light against his skin. His heart shifted off its rhythm.

"You need to support her head."

Her shoulder bumped against his chest as she placed the delicate bundle in his arms. The top of her head swept beneath his nose, offering him a whiff of whatever shampoo she used. It reminded him of summertime and his mom's strawberry shortcake. His mouth watered.

"I'm not sure this is a good idea." But his protest came too late. Grace lay along his forearm, her tiny body swaddled from chin to toes. The baby couldn't move, much less roll off his arm, but Keaton rested his right palm lightly on top of her.

"You doing okay?" Lark's soft lips wore a slight smile as she watched him cradle Grace.

"Fine." As long as she didn't fuss or move, he'd be great.

"I'll understand if you tell me you can't do this," Lark said. "Taking care of a baby is hard work."

"I'm not afraid of hard work." Keaton suspected she wanted him to back out. That was the last thing he was going to do. "I can do this. I just have to get used to how small she is."

"You do have rather large hands." Lark touched Grace's cheek with a fingertip. Her hand grazed his, making his skin tingle. "They make her look smaller than she is. But she's stronger than you might think."

He had a hard time believing that. Grace picked that second to yawn hugely and open her eyes. Her gaze latched on to his face, the expression wide and startled. Keaton stared back, mesmerized, until her eyes shut again. It wasn't until that happened that he realized his heart was thudding erratically.

Expecting Lark to laugh at his inexperience, he was surprised to find that she'd moved off several feet. Panic flared for a second. He noticed that Lark was watching him, gauging how he handled the situation. He was far out of his comfort zone. *Relax,* he told himself. He had to appear comfortable being alone with his niece if he was going to convince Lark that he could take care of the delicate infant.

He shifted Grace a little, learning the feel of her. Once again the baby opened her eyes. This time she let out a strange little grunt. Keaton didn't know if that was normal or not. He needed to do some research on preemies. A little knowledge would go a long way toward making him feel more confident.

"You really don't need to do this," Lark said, coming up alongside him once more.

"Yes, I do." He shoved aside any lingering doubts about his ability to take care of such a tiny baby. "She grunts."

"I noticed that. Might have something to do with her acid reflux issues. A lot of preemies suffer from it. Luckily Grace isn't too bad."

Another thing for him to worry about. Damn Jake. Where the hell was his brother? Skye and Grace were his responsibility. Keaton stared down at the sleeping baby. Jake's unavailability disturbed him. It wasn't like his brother to go off the grid. Something bad must have happened, but Keaton didn't have a clue where to start looking.

"Here, let me take her." Lark had stepped into his space once more.

Keaton liked how his body reacted to her nearness. Since Skye's accident and Grace's birth, he'd been at the hospital at least a couple times a week to check on them. He'd had plenty of time to notice Lark and indulge his curiosity about her.

"I've got her."

"But she needs to be changed." She gave him an assessing look. "Have you ever changed a baby before?"

"No. And before you say anything, let me point out that I intend to learn everything there is about taking care of a baby before you have to go back to work."

"Everything?" She looked doubtful.

"Everything."

"Why do I believe you?"

"Because like you, I graduated at the top of my class?"

Her lack of surprise at his declaration told Keaton that she'd known this about him. Logic told him her confidence in him would grow if she understood he brought intelligence as well as determination to the table.

"I suppose just about everything can be found on the internet these days," she agreed.

"So, are you going to walk me through changing her?" Keaton ignored the voice inside his head warning him how tiny and fragile Grace was. If he let any nervousness show, he'd never convince Lark to let him help.

"If that's what you want."

"It's what I want."

Two

The ranch house where Lark and Skye had grown up was a sprawling single-story structure with a cathedral ceiling over the enormous, open great room. Lark's father was an avid hunter, and the walls between the windows and ceiling were covered with trophies of white-tailed deer and bobwhite quail.

Above the dining table hung a chandelier made of antlers. A second one hung above the living room seating area composed of a brown leather couch and love seat. A fire crackled in the fireplace. Set into a sixteen-by-fourteen foot wall and surrounded by large river rock, it took up a corner of the room. As usual the television was on. Lark could tell her father wasn't home because it wasn't tuned to a sports program. Instead her mother had on the shopping channel.

Lark's rubber-soled shoes made no sound on the tile as she went across the room, shrugged out of her wool coat and draped it over one of the dining chairs. Her mother was in the open kitchen. Lark tried to gauge her mother's mood as she drew near.

"Oh, Lark. Must you wear those scrubs? They do nothing for your figure. And you really should do something about those dark circles under your eyes. They're not attractive."

Having just come from a double shift at the hospital because Marsha had called in sick again, Lark couldn't summon the energy to explain why she looked so tired. "Is that a new lipstick?" she asked. It made her mother happy to talk about herself, and Lark needed her in a good mood.

Vera Taylor smiled, obviously pleased that her daughter had noticed. "Passion's Promise." She dug into her purse and pulled out a tube. "It might be a good shade for you. Come closer and let me see."

Fighting down impatience, Lark let her mother apply the vivid red, knowing it would look ridiculous on her. She rarely wore make-up at all, much less something as eye-catching as ruby lipstick.

"And a little concealer." Her daughter's docility

had prompted Vera to pull a bag of make-up out of her purse. It was a rare mother-daughter bonding moment. Skye had been the pretty one, the one Vera could relate to. "Some color in your cheeks."

Vera stepped back and regarded her daughter with something akin to satisfaction. Lark's chest constricted. No matter how much she loved her mother, Lark had never been completely sure her mother felt the same way about her. Vera's childhood in San Antonio had been composed of a string of beauty pageants starting when she was one. She'd grown up praised for her beauty and style. Lark was sure it had broken her heart to give birth to a child of average prettiness and no interest in fashion.

Her mother must have thanked heaven when Skye came along. Beautiful and personable, with an abundance of talent. A mini Vera. A doll for her to dress and mold into the perfect pageant princess.

"See, that took me no more than a minute and a half and you look so much better. Imagine what would happen if we did a little mascara and eye shadow. You really should take more care with your appearance. What will people think?"

Considering that her patients in the ICU were unconscious and their family members too distressed to notice anything but their loved ones, Lark doubted that it mattered what she looked like. "I'll make more of an effort."

Knowing it would make her mother happy, Lark went into the small bathroom off the entry and checked her appearance. To her amazement, her mother was right. The little bit of makeup had transformed her. She was pretty. Not beautiful like Skye or their mother, but maybe attractive enough to make Keaton give her a second look?

The instant the thought entered her head, Lark banished it. Depending on how her mother responded to Lark's request to babysit Grace, she might just be stuck dealing with Keaton on a much more regular basis. If that happened, the last thing she needed was to start wondering if she appealed to him.

First of all, there was the hundred and some years of fighting between their families.

Then there was the little problem of whether or not she could trust him. Skye had put her faith in Jake and look what had happened. He'd vanished when she needed him most.

Last, but certainly not least, Keaton's brusque manner and ruggedness were a little overwhelming. Granted, he'd handled Grace with an acceptable amount of gentleness, but he'd obviously been on his best behavior. Would he be as careful with her?

And would she want him to be?

Swept away by the thought of his large hands skimming over her body, pulling her tight against him as his mouth claimed hers in a vigorous kiss, Lark shuddered in delight. Her skin warmed as the fantasy heated her blood. She could almost feel the scrape of his rough chin against her neck. Desire lanced through her like an electric shock, leaving her knees oddly unsteady.

"Mom," she called, emerging from the bathroom. "I have a favor to ask you."

Vera frowned. "I'm not sure this is a good time. Your father is very distressed about the loss of the tree farm and the damage done to the irrigation pipes."

Lark recognized this tactic. Her mother was always using Tyrone as an excuse to avoid doing things she deemed too great a burden. Ignoring her mother's broad hint, Lark muscled on.

"Grace gets to leave the hospital in a couple days."

"So soon?"

"It's been three months."

And as far as Lark knew, Vera had only stopped by once. Lark thought about Keaton's mom, visiting both a child she didn't fully believe was her granddaughter and the woman who'd been instrumental in taking her son away. Gloria had just as much reason to take her anger out on Skye and the baby, but she'd chosen a path of forgiveness instead.

"Things have been so bad around here, I haven't noticed how much time has passed."

"I was wondering if you could help me out with her."

"I don't know how I can find the time. There's so much to do here."

Lark braced herself to beg. Her parents had always made it hard for her to ask for anything. "Please, Mom. Can't you help me out until Skye gets better?"

"Are you sure you're the best one to be taking care of your sister's baby, Lark?"

"If not me, who else?"

"There's the father." Vera arched one perfectly shaped eyebrow. "Has he shown up yet?"

"If you mean Jake…" She didn't dare defend a Holt to her mother. "I don't know where he is. His brother hasn't had any luck locating him."

"Does that surprise you? None of those people can be trusted."

"Grace is a Taylor, Mom." Lark wasn't comfortable misleading her mother, but she hoped that maybe Vera would be more inclined to help if the conflict with the Holts wasn't part of the equation. "None of us had heard from Skye in four years. We don't even know if she and Jake were still together."

Vera considered this and for a brief second, Lark thought her mother might have forgiven how badly Skye hurt them when she'd run off with a Holt. But then Vera shook her head.

"I heard that brother of his is doing a DNA test. We'll know soon enough, won't we?"

"Grace is so beautiful, Mom," Lark said, hoping if she appealed to what her mother valued most that Vera might be persuaded to put aside her hurt and embrace her granddaughter. "She looks exactly like Skye." Which wasn't completely true, but hopefully Vera would be so thrilled to have a mini Skye to smother with love that she wouldn't notice the Holt eyes and bone structure.

"I'm sure she's quite lovely." Vera could have been speaking of a stranger's child for all the warmth she showed. "I can see that you are quiet passionate about taking on the responsibility of your sister's baby. I just don't think you realize how challenging it will be with you working full-time. A normal baby is exhausting and she's bound to have special needs. I'll speak with your father about helping you out with the child care costs."

And Lark knew her last hope was gone. Her mother wasn't ready to forgive Skye for turning her back on her family and would resist warming up to Grace.

"I don't want a stranger taking care of her," she told her mother, letting her disappointment show. It was looking pretty certain that her options had dwindled to Keaton.

"She's had strangers taking care of her for the last three months," Vera retorted a touch impatiently. "I don't see the difference."

The difference was Grace had needed medical attention and the nurses in the NICU were experts in the care of preemies. "I appreciate your offer of financial help, but I really think we owe it to Skye to do the best we can for Grace, and that means having her *family* take care of her."

A layer of frost coated Vera's features at Lark's mild reproof. Almost immediately she wished she could take back her criticism. No purpose would be served by alienating her mother, but along with regret, Lark noticed a tiny buzz of triumph for having stood up to her mother.

Unfortunately, Lark's confidence quickly faded as the reality of her situation engulfed her, and she drove home in such a state of disappointment that she didn't remember Keaton had invited himself on her shopping trip for the baby until she noticed the four-door pickup parked in front of her house.

The clock on her dashboard said quarter after two. She was fifteen minutes late. Lark settled her car in the garage and headed down the driveway to meet up with Keaton.

"I forgot we were getting together today."

"You look different." His eyes narrowed as he surveyed her.

When his gaze settled on her lips, Lark remembered the makeup her mother had applied. "I went to ask my mother for help with Grace. She thought I looked tired so she put makeup on me."

"You look very nice."

"Thank you."

Nice wasn't beautiful, but it was better than tired and drawn. And there was something new about the way he stared at her. Something intense and interested that made her pay attention to the flutters in her stomach and the slow heat building in her core.

"Are you heading back to work?" He indicated her scrubs.

Lark shook her head. The slight breeze cooled her skin. "One of my coworkers called in sick and we're shorthanded as it is. I pulled a double shift." A sharp wind cut off any further explanation she might have made. "Do you want to come inside?"

"I picked up a few things this morning. I'll go get them."

"You did?" Lark wasn't sure whether to be pleased

or dismayed. He was really determined to take care of Grace.

From the backseat of the pickup he unloaded two enormous bags printed with the logo of the local baby store. Lark hastened to open her front door so he could carry his bundles inside.

"What is all this?"

"Bedding, clothes." Keaton followed Lark into her living room and deposited everything on her couch. He glanced around. "I know you said you hadn't bought a crib yet. I thought that was something we could do together."

Curiosity drove her to investigate what he'd chosen. Rather than an ultra-feminine pastel-pink ensemble, he'd chosen pale yellow sheets, bumper, dust ruffle and comforter with fun jungle animals. Lark spied pajamas, bodysuits and pants, tiny socks, bibs and a towel.

"You look surprised," Keaton said.

"I am. You did a great job. How did you know what to buy?"

"I went online and found a list for what to have on hand when bringing home a baby."

"She'll need some diapers. I can get those later today."

"I already contacted a diaper service."

"I figured we would just use disposables."

"Cloth is better for the environment."

She couldn't argue with that. "I wasn't sure I wanted to deal with keeping dirty diapers around until they could be picked up." And the unpleasantness that went along with doing that.

"The person I spoke with said they have a hamper that keeps the smell contained."

"Sounds like you've done your research."

"I always do."

Lark was surprised at the resentment brewing in her gut. Why was she annoyed with Keaton for being helpful? After she'd worked back-to-back shifts, she should be relieved that some of the preparations for Grace's homecoming were done. So what if she wasn't the smartest person in the room?

Thinking of her double shift reminded Lark just how tired she was. Before she could contain it, an enormous yawn broke free.

"Sorry."

"You're tired."

"Back-to-back shifts are brutal."

"I can take care of the shopping and get the crib. I'm sure you have a list of everything you still need to do before Grace leaves the hospital."

While she realized he was only trying to lend a hand, Lark rebelled at the thought of him taking over the preparations. Grace was her responsibility. If she was too tired to shop for her, how was she going to cope once her niece came home?

"No." Lark gave her head a vehement shake. "I want to pick out the crib and finish up the shopping. It won't take long. And you're right. I have a list of what I need."

She should be annoyed that he'd presumed things about her habits when he knew nothing about her, but she found herself flattered by his accurate read. Few people noticed her much less paid attention to her practices.

A glow bloomed in her chest, banishing her tiredness. She recognized Keaton as the source of her abrupt sense of well-being. His proximity had a disturbing effect on her world. Long ago she'd learned that asking for help was likely to end up in a rebuff. So she'd grown used to muddling along without anyone noticing she needed help much less offering to pitch in. Now she had Keaton insisting on lightening her load and was more than a little afraid to trust what he was offering.

Dropping her gaze to the floor, she said, "I'll be okay on my own."

Stubborn, Keaton noted, just like her father. She was determined to make things more difficult for herself rather than let him help. Pushing down his irritation, he said, "Why don't I put this stuff away while you change?"

"I'll take care of it." She drew near and reached out for the bags. "I'm going to put the crib in my room. The master suite is on the opposite side of the house from the other two bedrooms, and I don't want her so far away."

Keaton surrendered the purchases and watched her retreat. As soon as she was out of sight he surveyed his surroundings. The house was a split-floor plan, just as she'd described, with bedrooms on opposite sides of an expansive great room/dining room/kitchen combination. The design was modern; the open flow of the place made it nice for entertaining.

The rooms reflected exactly what he'd expected her style to be. Like him, she preferred furniture that was comfortable rather than stylish. She'd always struck him as practical, but she'd chosen dreamy Texas landscapes for her walls.

Books overflowed the shelves that flanked the fireplace, leaving no room for knickknacks. Or family photos. More books were stacked on the coffee table and each of the side tables. Which wasn't surprising: his every memory of her had a book in it.

One of the most telling aspects of her décor, and where their taste was drastically different, was the lack of electronics of any kind. That included a television, stereo and video equipment. As rustic as his cabin was, one of the first purchases he'd made before moving in was a forty-inch TV. How could she stand not having such an important connection to the outside world?

"Is something wrong?"

Keaton turned his head and spied her coming his way. She'd traded baggy scrubs for snug jeans that hugged her curves and a dark green sweater with a scoop neck that showed a hint of cleavage.

Knowing he was staring at her in mouthwatering fascination, but unable to help himself, Keaton answered her question. "You don't have a television."

"No." She knotted a scarf around her neck, slipped into her coat and gathered up her purse and keys.

"Any particular reason?" With the most seductive aspects of her form hidden from view, Keaton was able to wrestle his thoughts back into line.

"What's the point?"

"It's television."

She focused a sharp gaze on him. "Mindless entertainment. I prefer to read or bake. I like feeling productive."

"Not everything on TV is mindless. There are educational programs." After gesturing her to go first through the doorway, Keaton stepped aside so she could lock the front door. "Some interesting stuff."

"I'll take your word for it," she murmured, looking completely unconvinced as he opened the passenger door for her.

His pulse kicked up as she whisked past him. Was his attraction for her going to cause problems? She was already as skittish as a feral cat. If she got any inkling that he craved a taste of her lips, it might ruin the fragile cease-fire they'd established.

Keaton slid behind the wheel. Although he wasn't much for small talk, he thought engaging Lark in casual conversation would be a good way to build rapport. "You have quite a collection of books. What do you like to read?"

"I alternate between classics and contemporary fiction."

Hearing her answer, he sighed in frustration. Their taste in books wasn't going to keep the dialogue flowing easily. "I like biographies and nonfiction."

She nodded and subsided into silence. Keaton shot her a sideways glance and noticed that she was gripping her purse as if it was a lifeline. He wanted her to relax in his company. If she decided he wasn't the villain her father made him out to be, he would have an easier time staking his own claim on Grace.

Tapping his fingers on the steering wheel, Keaton tried again. "I downloaded a couple books on preemies to my e-reader in an attempt to figure out what to expect with Grace."

"At this point her gestational age is that of a newborn. She's still tiny compared to most, but her need for specialized care is done."

"I realize that I missed being around for her early days, but the books talked about kangaroo care where the baby is held against her mother's skin to help with her development."

Lark nodded. "Because she couldn't leave the NICU, I would go in before and after my shift and hold her like that." Her voice took on a husky note. "I wish we could have put her and Skye together, but I did the best I could."

"You did a great job," he assured her. "She's thriving and ready to leave the NICU." Once again it struck Keaton just how much Lark had been dealing with on her own, and irritation with his brother flared anew. Whatever Lark and Grace needed, he would make sure they were taken care of. "But I think you've single-handedly shouldered the burden for too long. From everything I've read, preemies are more work than an average newborn, which means you're going to be even more exhausted. Let me help."

"I would be lying if I told you I was completely convinced of my ability to take care of Grace on my own. Frankly, I'm terrified of failing. I owe it to Skye to do what is best for Grace."

The level of conviction in Lark's voice resonated with Keaton.

"That's exactly what I'm trying to do for Jake." And in his brother's absence, he intended to protect Jake's rights. The Taylors needed to understand that Grace was also a Holt—Keaton was convinced of that, with or without the DNA test—and that they had an equal say in her care.

"We share a common goal, then." She stared hard at the road before them. "I'm sorry if I've been suspicious of your motives, but I have to tell you that all my life I've had to listen to how untrustworthy your family is."

"It's not true."

"I'm sure where the rest of the world is concerned it's not, but when it comes to my family, there's been so much strife over the years I can't shake my uneasiness. And then there's the fact that I haven't spoken with Skye since she left Royal. I don't know what happened between her and Jake. I don't know if I'm doing the right thing letting you be involved with Grace."

He wasn't sure what had happened between Skye

and Lark, but he had a feeling the Taylor-Holt feud had caused the sisters' relationship to suffer the same the way his and Jake's had. Whatever had happened, there was no question that Lark bore her sister no lasting ill will. Her dedication to Skye and Grace was unflinching.

"I assure you—" His phone began to ring before he could finish the thought. Not recognizing the number, he keyed the truck's hands-free option and answered the call. "Keaton Holt."

"Mr. Holt, this is Sabrina from Dr. Boyle's office." The doctor who had administered the DNA test.

Keaton glanced Lark's way and spied her somber green eyes on him. "What are the results?"

"The kinship index was well over 1.0. You and Grace show a strong chance of being related. That's a very good indication that your brother is her father."

Because they hadn't been able to collect Jake's DNA, they'd had to test Skye and Keaton for an uncle comparison. It wasn't as definitive as a paternity test, but the results were strong and should satisfy all but the most skeptical.

"Thank you, Sabrina. Please send the results to me by email."

"Of course, Mr. Holt. And congratulations."

Keaton ended the call and waited for Lark's reaction. They were nearing the furniture store where she intended to get Grace's crib. In a minute there would be no time for private discussion.

"That's it, then," she said, her voice low and without inflection.

"You don't sound surprised."

"Grace looks like Jake."

Her admission annoyed him. "But you fought me on the DNA test."

"I didn't want to believe my sister and her baby had been abandoned by your brother." Her eyes hardened. "How could he be so unreachable? They need him."

"They have us," Keaton reminded her. "I'm going to do everything in my power to take care of my niece. And your sister."

"I spoke with my mother today. She and my dad are busy because of the damaged tree farm and other things." She ducked her head, her posture defeated. "I think I'm going to need help taking care of Grace."

He was saddened, but not surprised, that the Taylors had chosen not to pitch in to care for their granddaughter. Skye had been disowned by her parents when she left with Jake. The Taylors were obstinate and inflexible. It was their intolerance that had forced their daughter to run away from Royal and further aggravate an already bitter war between their families.

He wanted to touch Lark's hand, to reassure her that he was on her side. "You and I are going to make a great team."

"That remains to be seen," she remarked, some of her prickliness returning. "I'm dreading the scene when my parents find out you and I are working together to care for Grace."

If that bothered her, she was really going to hate where his thoughts had taken him over the last twenty-four hours. "You're doing the right thing for Grace, and that's what counts."

"I hate having to choose between being a good daughter and a good sister and aunt." Lark worried her fingers along her jacket's zipper. "I suppose you think it's stupid that a twenty-seven-year-old woman is afraid of upsetting her parents."

From what he'd experienced of Tyrone Taylor's temper, Keaton understood Lark's desire to avoid her father's wrath.

He guided the truck into the furniture store parking lot and took a spot not far from the front door. Keaton shut off the engine and sat in silence for a long moment. He was overwhelmed by a strong desire to protect her from anyone who made her unhappy, but she wouldn't appreciate his opinion about her parents even if all he was doing was defending her.

At last he spoke. "We can't let this rift between our families keep us from doing what is best for Grace."

"You're absolutely right." She nodded fiercely. "Let's go buy some baby furniture."

If Keaton had expected to spend the next two hours bored to tears while Lark shopped, he was pleasantly surprised when she went straight to a crib in the middle row and gave it a quick nod.

"I want this one," she told the sales clerk who approached less than a minute later. "As well as that changing table."

"I'll get it all written up. When do you want it delivered?"

"The sooner the better."

"Let me check the schedule. We have tomorrow afternoon available."

Lark frowned. "I have to work."

"That will be fine," Keaton said.

"But I won't be home."

"I'll meet them." He could see immediately that she was uncomfortable with the idea. "You might as well get used to having me in your house. I'm going to be taking care of Grace there, after all."

"You're right." Lark shook her head. "I haven't

had to share my space with anyone since buying my house two years ago."

"You're never lonely being on your own?"

"Sometimes." She offered him a tiny smile. "Mostly I love it. I walk in my front door and don't have to worry about anyone but me."

"Bringing Grace home is going to change that."

"I don't mean it the way it sounds. It's just that with Skye coming home, my parents are stressed out and things around the hospital have been really challenging since the tornado. I moved from the surgery team to ICU so I could be closer to Skye and am having a hard time with the nurses I'm working with. Everything I say gets twisted around. I feel as if I'm constantly walking on eggshells. It's exhausting."

"Sounds like you need a break."

"I'm taking a week off when Grace comes home." She gave a happy sigh. "I'll need it to get her settled in."

With the crib paid for and the delivery arrangements finalized, Keaton and Lark headed back to his truck. He scanned Lark's face as she buckled herself in. She looked worn to the bone.

"Can I buy you dinner before I take you home?"

She gave him a weary smile. "I'm too tired to be much company."

"How about takeout?"

"Are you always this persistent?"

Yes, when something was important to him, and Lark's well-being was rapidly climbing his priority list. "I don't feel right taking you home without feeding you."

Besides, he wanted to spend more time in her company. She intrigued him. They'd been neighbors most of their lives, their families had been at odds with each other for generations. He knew little about her beyond what was common knowledge, but had long harbored a sense that they could be kindred spirits if circumstances were different.

"Obviously you are not going to take no for an answer and I'm too tired to argue." She leaned her head against the back of the seat and closed her eyes. "But just because I gave in this once, don't think you can get your way every time."

He felt a smile tug at his lips as he started the car, but refrained from pointing out that ninety-nine percent of the time people did as he indicated because he was right. She'd figure that out soon enough.

Three

"I'm taking Grace home today," Lark told her comatose sister as she finished up her last shift for a week. "I hope you're okay with that. She's ready to leave and I'm her closest relative."

The closest one that wanted her, anyway.

"I wish we could get in contact with Jake and let him know about you and Grace. It would be nice if you could wake up and tell us where he is." She paused as her throat closed up.

The hope that Lark had clung to while her sister's coma had been medically induced had wavered in the days since the doctor had taken Skye off the Pentobarbital and she hadn't awakened. As a medical professional, Lark was well aware her sister's chances of ever waking diminished with each day that passed.

A couple deep breaths allowed her to go on. "Since Jake hasn't shown up yet, Keaton has offered to help me take care of her. We're going to trade off watching her at my house. Since the tornado demolished the Holt family ranch house, he's been living in a hunting cabin on the property and I'm sure it's no place for Grace."

Lark fussed with the sheet that covered Skye, hating her sister's stillness. Skye had always been so vivacious. So beautiful. So outgoing and personable. So not like Lark. Sometimes she wondered if they were really sisters or if one of them was the victim of a switched-at-birth scenario.

Skye's golden hair looked lank and listless against her pale skin. There were shadows beneath her closed eyes. After three months in the hospital the bruises and scrapes that had marred her face and arms were long healed, as was her left earlobe, probably torn during the same impact that had caused her head wound. She'd lost the diamond out of her earring, but the screw back had kept the stud in place. The hospital had given Skye's jewelry to Lark for safekeeping, and because Skye's phone and luggage had never been recovered, the earrings were her only possession. The lack of any sort of ring continued to dismay Lark. What had happened between Skye and Jake these last four years?

"I bought her a crib and a changing table," Lark continued. "Keaton picked up her bedding. All by himself. It's really cute. Yellow with jungle animals. I set up the furniture in my sitting area, but it's pretty cramped. For the time being, I'm going to keep her in a bassinet. I think she'll feel more secure in a smaller space. Eventually I'll transition her to the crib. Or you can just wake up and take care of that yourself."

Holding her breath was fruitless and silly, but Lark issued the challenge at least once a day and hoped that her sister would respond.

"I don't want to fail you," she whispered. "I did four years ago and I've regretted it every day since." Lark wiped at a trace of moisture at the corner of her eye. "Did I mention what an annoying know-it-all Keaton is?" She needed to change the subject or risk further tears. "He seems to think if he researches something thoroughly enough that he becomes an expert."

A smile tugged at Lark's lips as she recalled how he'd looked the first time he held Grace. "And he's bossy. He decided that we were going to use a diaper service instead of disposable. Didn't even consult me. Of course, I like the idea that we won't be loading up the landfill, but I should have at least been given an opportunity to agree."

The wife of Skye's nearest neighbor came to visit. Her husband was suffering from sepsis, and his condition had been touch-and-go for the last week. Lark was happy to see he'd turned a corner toward recovery.

"I'd better get going," she murmured to Skye. "I'm supposed to meet Keaton in a few minutes. I'll bring Grace by to see you before we leave and then visit in a few days once I'm sure she's settling in okay and that Keaton is comfortable taking care of her. Before this he hadn't had any experience with babies, and I think he's intimidated by how tiny Grace is. But he's been handling her quite a bit these last few days and I'm surprised how deftly he manages her diaper and dressing her."

With a last squeeze of Skye's hand, Lark left the ICU. She waved to her coworkers as she walked by the nurses' station, but only Jessa gave her a smile and it was quickly gone. As Lark rode the elevator to the pediatric floor, she wasn't surprised how relieved she felt to have a weeklong break from the ICU nurses.

From the beginning they'd mistaken her shyness for superiority and now did everything in their power to shun her. Lark had a hard enough time opening up to people without having to overcome hostility.

As she stepped out of the elevator, it occurred to her that she'd never felt the least bit shy or uneasy with Keaton. The feud between their families should have made her anxious around him, yet from the moment she'd run into him in the hospital, she felt as if they'd known each other for years. Weird when he was the son of her parents' enemy. Or maybe she felt the connection more closely because of the bad blood between their families. Heaven knew she'd thought about him often enough. Him and Jake. Especially after Skye ran off with Jake and Lark spent a lot of time wondering what was so special about a Holt that would cause her sister to choose him over her family.

Her pulse kicked up a notch as she approached the NICU, but she didn't see Keaton. A glance at the clock showed it was fifteen minutes before their agreed-on meeting time. She'd caught a ride to the hospital with Julie. Since she was taking Grace home after her shift, Keaton was giving her and the baby a ride home. When Lark assured him she would be fine on her own, he'd insisted on being there. His steely determination had left her torn between relief and annoyance.

Lark approached Grace's basinet. She was wearing a pink dress one of the NICU nurses had crocheted. A matching pink headband encircled her head. This wasn't a normal practice, but nothing about Grace's situation had been normal thus far and Lark was one of their own.

"Thank you all so much," Lark said to her colleagues as she blinked back a rush of tears that flooded her eyes. "You've taken such great care of Grace."

"If you need anything or have any questions," Amy, the senior NICU nurse said, "just call."

"Thanks." She'd grown accustomed to leaning on each of these women for support and guidance. It was terrifying to be heading out on her own.

Except she wasn't alone. Keaton would be there to help her. Her skin prickled. She hadn't quite gotten used to the idea that he would be spending time in her private space. Buying a house and living alone for the first time in her life had been blissful. No more worrying about saying the wrong thing to her roommate's friends or hearing their whispers and knowing they were talking about the weird girl who rarely came out of the second bedroom.

"You're going to do great," said Nancy. The nurse with the most experience in the NICU, she'd been the one Lark had turned to about her anxiety.

"I don't know why I'm so emotional." Lark

laughed self-consciously. At the hospital she worked hard to appear confident. Letting anyone glimpse her shy awkwardness might make them question her ability to do her job. "I guess I'm feeling a little overwhelmed."

"Oh, honey." Nancy wrapped her arm around Lark's shoulder and gave her a squeeze. "With your sister in a coma and this precious baby still so delicate, you've got a lot on your plate. Frankly, we'd be surprised if you weren't feeling that way."

Through the NICU's large window, Lark spotted Keaton. Her pulse gave a little leap as their eyes met. He nodded in acknowledgement, his grave expression and compelling gaze easing her turmoil a little. His presence reminded her that she wasn't alone.

Amy spoke up. "And it looks like Keaton Holt is going to be a big help." Her tone was sly, matching her wicked grin. "It's nice to see you two could put aside your families' differences."

Had they? Lark wasn't sure. A lifetime of hostility and accusations stood between them. Just because she and Keaton weren't at war with each other didn't mean they were going to get along. He was determined to the point of obstinacy and laser-focused when he decided he wanted something. While it might make him a successful rancher, it made fighting with him an exhausting enterprise. Lark tore her attention away from the tall, imposing ranch owner and redirected her thoughts to the five-pound bundle she held. For Grace's sake she and Keaton were just going to have to play nice.

Telling her pulse to settle down, Lark cradled Grace in her arms and gazed around the NICU for the last time. Burdened with a well-stocked diaper bag and the responsibility of her delicate charge, she threw back her shoulders and walked the gantlet of smiling nurses who'd gathered to wish her and Grace well.

"How is Grace this morning?" Keaton asked as she approached.

"Doing better than I am." Lark shifted her grip on the baby as Keaton slid the well-stocked diaper bag off her shoulder, lightening her load. "Thanks."

"Don't tell me you're nervous." His genuine surprise bolstered her confidence.

"I owe it to Skye to make everything perfect for Grace."

"It will be."

The hand he set on her back caused a shiver of awareness to travel up her spine. His touch was at once reassuring and stimulating. She wanted to lean into his strength. The urge gave her much to contemplate. For as long as Lark could remember she'd been a solo act. Growing up, she'd enjoyed solitude. Smart and independent, she'd been neither a leader nor a follower, but one of those quirky types who loved books and was perfectly content doing her own thing. Looking back, Lark wasn't sure if her isolation had been the cause or the result of her social awkwardness.

"If you don't mind, I'd like to stop by the ICU before we leave the hospital," Lark said as they walked down the hall to the elevators. "This is Grace's first time outside the NICU, and I want her to see her mother before we leave."

Lark didn't add that she was hoping that Grace's presence would somehow miraculously awaken Skye from her coma.

"Of course."

As always, she was discouraged by the sight of her beautiful, vibrant sister lying so still, the only sign of life the beep and electronic readouts coming from the machines that measured her vitals. But Lark's reaction today was worse than normal. Her throat closed up as misery swamped her. What if Skye never woke up? What if Grace never got to know how amazing her mother was?

"Damn," she muttered, wiping away the moisture that escaped the corners of her eyes. "I'm sorry," she said to Keaton.

"For what? Being sad that your sister is like this? It's terrible."

She wanted to smile in appreciation of his understanding, but her facial muscles were controlled by the ache in her heart, so she settled for a nod.

"Skye, this is Grace. You haven't had a chance to meet her because she's been too tiny to leave the NCIU. She's so beautiful. I wish you would open your eyes and see for yourself." Staying away from the wires that connected Skye to the monitors, Lark fitted Grace into the hollow between her sister's arm and her side. "She needs her mommy."

As soon as Lark finished speaking, Grace punched outward with both fists and opened her eyes. Lark half expected her face to screw up in distress, but the baby blinked and relaxed in a way that Lark had never seen before. Was it being snuggled against her mother for the first time in three months?

Keaton leaned forward to peer at Grace. His shoulder pressed against Lark's back. "She looks happy."

"The mother-daughter bond is alive and well."

How comfortable it would be to rest her head against his broad chest and pull his muscular arms around her body. The longing for his touch was so compelling, Lark had to dig her fingernails into her palms to keep from acting on the impulse. What was happening to her? She'd never been so physically drawn to a man before. Usually the men she dated were intellectually stimulating, but not exactly fantasy material. Not that they were unattractive, but their allure had been mostly cerebral.

Grace yawned and her eyes drifted shut. She knuckled one cheek. Her other hand rested on her mother's arm.

The anxious knot in Lark's chest tightened. "What if Skye never wakes up?" It was the first time she'd spoken the fear out loud.

"She will." Keaton's big hands settled on her shoulders. "As Grace gets stronger, so will her mother."

Keaton's words couldn't have been any more perfect. Lark's optimism surged.

"You're right." As much as she was loathed to disrupt the rapport that had bloomed between her and Keaton, she needed to get Grace home and settled. "Say goodbye to your mommy," she said to the baby, lifting her away from Skye. It hurt Lark's heart to separate mother and daughter, but she told herself it was only temporary. Before she left Skye's bedside, Lark turned to Keaton. "I want you to know how much I appreciate everything you've done. I realized this morning that I'd underestimated how much I needed to get ready for Grace's homecoming. I couldn't have done it without you."

Her father would be furious to hear her say those words. But if he and her mother refused to step up and be grandparents to Grace, they had no right to criticize Lark for accepting Keaton's assistance. Unfortunately that wouldn't stop them from bombarding her with their opinions. Lark cringed away from thinking about her father's ire. Always volatile where the Holts were concerned, he'd become a powder keg since the tornado leveled his tree farm.

"You don't need to thank me," Keaton said. "We're doing this for Grace, remember?"

"For Grace," she agreed.

With Keaton a step behind her, Lark headed out of the ICU. As she neared the door to the hall, two people came into view. Her parents. They stood at the nurses' station, speaking with Lark's coworker Jessa and hadn't spotted Lark or Keaton yet.

She slowed her pace, all too aware of Keaton's towering presence behind her. In the rush of getting prepared for Grace's homecoming, Lark had neglected to mention to her parents that Keaton would be helping her with Grace. Or maybe she'd dodged the issue to put off dealing with her father's ire as long as possible. Lark gathered a breath to bolster her courage. This encounter promised to get ugly.

Her mother spotted her first. "Lark?" Her gaze bounced from her daughter to the man shadowing her. "What's going on?"

At Vera's sharp tone, Tyrone Taylor glanced around. His expression twisted with disgust when he saw Keaton.

"Grace is coming home with me today," Lark explained, stopping a good fifteen feet away from her parents, hoping distance and a soothing tone would keep her father's temper from flaring. "I brought her to see Skye before we left."

"And him?" Lark's father demanded. "What's he doing here?"

"I'm driving Lark and Grace home." Keaton's level reply was neither defensive nor aggressive. His body radiated calm confidence at Lark's side, but her tension didn't ease.

Lark had let Keaton take on the role of Grace's caretaker because her parents hadn't stepped up. Was that dawning on Tyrone and Vera or were they too consumed by their needs and desires to realize they would never be nominated for grandparents of the year?

"Since when are you two so chummy?" Tyrone demanded, his attention fixed on his daughter.

Lark felt her chin lift to a defiant angle in response to her father's hostility. "Keaton is Grace's uncle. We are both concerned about her welfare." She glanced down at the tiny bundle of pink sweetness they all should be concerned about, but failed to refocus her father's attention.

"I don't know why you've accepted Jake as Grace's father. He sure as hell isn't acting like it. What sort of man abandons his baby and the woman he claims to love?" Tyrone shot Keaton a hard look. "What does your brother have to say for himself?"

"I haven't spoken with Jake."

Lark's father made a dismissive noise, but his next words were for Lark. "I told your sister four years ago that Jake was going to ruin her life."

"He hasn't."

"He forced her to turn her back on her family and now he's abandoned her."

"You don't know that he did," Keaton said. "I know my brother. He loves Skye. If he's not here, there's a good reason why."

"And none of that matters at this moment," Lark chimed in, modulating her voice so as not to disturb the sleeping infant. "Grace and Skye need all our love and support. That's where our energy should be focused." Frustration ate at her. She needed her father to put aside his dislike of all things Holt and concentrate on what was best for his daughter and granddaughter. "We should get going. I need to get Grace home." In the spirit of putting differences aside, Lark added, "It would be great if you could come by later this week and have dinner. You could spend some time getting to know Grace."

"Maybe you should bring her out to the ranch instead," Tyrone countered, his hard gaze still resting on Keaton.

"Preemie's lungs are always delicate," Lark explained. "It will be better for Grace if she doesn't venture out for the first few weeks. That's why I wanted you to come over."

"Will he be there?"

"We'll check our schedule and let you know what works for us," Vera said in a rush, her response geared toward ending the conversation. She fussed with the numerous bracelets on her wrist and glanced at the clock on the wall. "Tyrone, I have a meeting with my nutritionist in forty-five minutes, so we'd better go see Skye before we run out of time."

Lark said goodbye to her parents and headed for the elevator. She didn't realize how much she'd been dreading running into them until she let out a huge breath.

Keaton shot her a somber glance. "You okay?"

"That could have gone so much worse."

* * *

Keaton agreed. But it should have gone a lot better.

For the first time in his life, Keaton was having difficulty keeping his opinion to himself. The reserve Tyrone and Vera demonstrated toward their daughters irritated him. It was one thing to dislike Jake, Keaton and their parents based on grievances that had plagued generations of Taylors and Holts over numerous decades. It was another to let that animosity drive a wedge between them and their lovely, successful daughters.

"It's cool outside," he remarked as they stepped off the elevator. "Why don't you wait in the lobby while I bring the car around?"

Lark settled into a seat by the door and he set the diaper bag beside the chair. Before he could leave, she stopped him with a light touch on his arm. "Keaton, I'm sorry about what my father said about Jake. My sister adored your brother."

He didn't like her use of the past tense. "I believe she still loves him. I don't know what's happened between them these last four years or why he's not here now, but until I know for certain that my message about Skye and Grace has gotten to him, I'm going to trust that they're still together and very much in love."

"I wish I had your faith."

Her melancholy expression weighed on him as he strode to the parking ramp where he'd left his car. Until he'd approached her about assisting with Grace's care, she'd never struck him as someone who needed help. Her competent exterior deflected anyone from noticing her vulnerability to harsh words and malicious intent.

Today, watching her in the NICU with the other nurses, seeing her anxiety, had cemented his perception of her as someone he should be taking care of.

The feeling had been building since the day he went with her to buy Grace's crib, working its way through his subconscious. Now it burst upon him like a solar flare.

Thanks to the land dispute between the Taylors and Holts she might not ever be his friend, but with Baby Grace's arrival, she'd become his family.

With this fresh insight firmly entrenched in his awareness, Keaton helped Lark settle Grace into her car seat for the ride home.

"I'm going to sit in the back with her," Lark said, fussing over the straps that secured the tiny infant.

"I'm sure she'll feel safe with you beside her." Keaton got behind the wheel and started the truck.

As the vehicle eased away from the curb, he worried over every bump in the road. "How is she doing?"

"Great. She's still asleep."

"Good." Silence reigned as Keaton concentrated on navigating the traffic around the hospital. Lark's house was a ten-minute drive, but it seemed to take twice that long. At last they arrived and began the process of releasing Grace from her safety seat. "I've been doing a lot of thinking about our situation in the last couple days," he began as Lark unlocked her front door and stepped inside. Keaton followed her with Grace nestled in his arms.

"What situation is that?"

The baby was starting to wake and Lark offered to take her, but Keaton shook his head. Now that he'd grown accustomed to how tiny and fragile she was, he liked snuggling her against his chest and watching her yawn and blink.

"The one where we trade off taking care of Grace."

"You've decided you're too busy to help out?" She set her hands on her hips and regarded him with resignation. "I think she's hungry."

"Then this is a great time for you to show me what goes into one of her bottles." He waited patiently until she spun on her heel and headed into the kitchen, and then he followed with Grace. He watched how Lark went about measuring the pow-dered formula and mixing it with water. "Most new mothers get to take off six to twelve weeks off work. You're only taking a week. I think you're going to need me around to do more than watch Grace while you're at the hospital."

Lark turned with the bottle in her hand and eyed him. "You don't think I can manage?"

"I think you will wear yourself to the bone try-ing to take care of Grace and Skye while working full time."

"My mother already offered to pay for a nanny and I refused."

Keaton saw the hurt in Lark's eyes and voiced the idea that had been cooking in his subconscious for several days. "I think I should move in here."

"Move in?"

It made perfect sense. Ever since the DNA re-sults came back he'd been contemplating how best to stake a claim on Grace for the sake of his brother and the Holt family. Moving in with Lark would prove he was as dedicated to his niece's welfare as she was.

"You demonstrated last week that your schedule is subject to change," he pointed out, seeing his logic was encroaching on her doubts.

"That's true, but it's not exactly as if you have a lot of time on your hands."

She was right about that. Between his regular duties at the ranch, the rebuilding efforts there and in town, he was stretched thin.

"Grace is my family. I'm going to do everything in my power to take care of her."

Lark exhaled tiredly. "I appreciate that you feel responsible, but you don't actually have to move in."

His muscles relaxed as he heard the beginnings of capitulation in her voice. "It would be better for you if I was here full-time."

"How do you figure?"

"Have you considered what will happen if Grace is up all night? If I'm here we can take turns getting up with her." He could see she was weakening. "It makes sense."

"Let me sleep on it tonight?" She held out her hands for the baby.

This time, Keaton gave up Grace. "Sure."

Only she never got the chance to sleep. Neither did Keaton. Shortly after Grace finished eating, she began to fuss.

"It's probably just a little gas," Lark explained, setting the infant on her shoulder and patting her back encouragingly. "Once she burps, she'll be fine."

But Grace wasn't fine and neither Lark nor

Keaton could get her to quiet. During the second hour of the baby's crying, Keaton got onto his tablet.

"She's dry, fed and obviously tired. Why won't she sleep?"

"Because it's her first day out of the NICU and she's overstimulated."

"It says here we can try white noise. Do you have a vacuum cleaner?"

Lark shot him a look. "It's in the laundry room." She pointed toward a door at the back of the kitchen.

Keaton plugged in the vacuum and turned it on. The hum acted like a swarm of bees against his eardrums, agitating him. If it had this effect on him, what must it be doing to a fussy baby? Closing the door behind him to muffle the sound, Keaton returned to the living room, where Lark paced and rocked Grace.

"Is it helping?" he asked, peering over her shoulder at his niece.

"I don't think so, but maybe we should give it a little time. She's pretty wound up at the moment."

But after an hour, it was obvious that the white noise was having no effect. Keaton returned to searching the internet for answers.

"How about wrapping her up?" he suggested. "Says here that babies feel more secure when they're swaddled." He cued up a video and watched it.

The demonstration looked straightforward, but the woman used a doll, not a real baby. "Give me Grace and watch this."

After several minutes, Lark set the tablet aside. "We can try it. I'll go see if I have a blanket that will work." She returned with two blankets of different sizes. "Hopefully one of these will do the trick."

As Keaton had feared, swaddling a live, unhappy baby was a lot harder than an unmoving doll.

Lark braced her hands on the dining room table and stared down at the swaddled baby. "This doesn't look right."

Keaton returned to the video. "I think we missed this part here."

Grace was growing more upset by the second and she'd managed to free her left arm.

"Is it terrible that I have no idea what I'm doing?" Lark sounded close to tears. It had been a long, stressful evening.

"Not at all. I think every first-time parent feels just as overwhelmed as we do right now."

"Thank you for sticking around and helping me."

"We're helping Grace."

The corners of Lark's lips quivered as she smiled. "Not very well, as it happens."

And then, because she looked determined and hopeless all at once, Keaton succumbed to the impulse that had been threatening to break free all week. He cupped her cheek, lowered his head and kissed her.

Four

The press of Keaton's lips against hers lasted all of ten seconds, but they were ten of the best seconds Lark had ever experienced. With his granite features and steely nature, she expected his lips would be stiff, his kisses firm and unyielding. Therefore she was caught off guard by the softness of his mouth, the luxurious press and pull as he captured her sighs.

For ten seconds her brain stopped and her body came alive.

Then Grace's insistent protests came between them like a wedge, bringing reality back.

"Let's try the swaddling again," Keaton suggested, his long black lashes obscuring his eyes from her as his hand fell away from her face. "I think I know where we went wrong."

The next try went much better, but it wasn't snug enough for Grace's taste. Lark stood beside Keaton, her body alive with raucous cravings, her mind numb with disbelief, and watched his big hands wrap the cloth around the flailing infant. His confidence had grown in the last couple hours as he'd taken his turn trying to calm Grace. Lark's belief in his abilities had increased, as well. She appreciated how he'd not just stood by helplessly and let her figure out what was wrong with Grace, but he'd taken to the internet to find a solution to soothe the infant.

"She's still not happy," he commented as soon as the last corner was tucked away, creating a cocoon.

"Maybe she just wants it to be tighter."

"Do you want to give it a try?"

Lark shook her head. Their kiss was too fresh. Her body had yet to come down off the thrill. She couldn't let him see how her hands trembled. "You're doing great."

He shot her a doubtful frown as he unwrapped Grace. Lark stood as close as she could to him without touching to observe his next attempt. Despite the lack of contact, energy arched across the distance between them, setting her skin to tingling.

"I think you could go a little tighter," she offered,

reaching out to demonstrate. Their hands brushed in passing, and the zap of contact caused her stomach muscles to tighten in reaction. She swallowed a gasp.

Fifteen minutes ago she'd decided to agree to his moving in. Now she wasn't so sure. Living in such close quarters was bound to lead to more inconsequential physical contact. And then there was that kiss to consider. She could easily write off Keaton's impulse as a reaction to the frustration of Grace's disquiet, but it hadn't been that sort of kiss. It had been tender and curious. He'd kissed Lark with focused deliberation as if that was the only thing on his mind. As if it had been on his mind for a while.

She trembled.

"I think we've finally got it right."

At Keaton's relieved words, Lark blinked and reoriented herself in the moment. The tight swaddle had done the trick. Grace had stopped crying and her mouth opened on a giant yawn.

"You did it."

"We did it," he corrected. "We're a team, remember?"

For the first time she didn't freeze up at his words. "A good team," she agreed, scooping the sleepy infant into her arms.

"I'm feeling more confident that we can do this."

Keaton followed her to the couch where the bassinet waited.

"You weren't before?"

"Not once she started crying and wouldn't stop."

Lark had begun having doubts way before they left the hospital. Taking care of her sister's baby was a responsibility Lark didn't take lightly. Add in Grace's premature birth and the risks that accompanied such things, and the need for success grew proportionately more crucial.

"It's been a long night," Lark said, placing Grace in the bassinet before sitting beside her. After she'd confirmed that Grace slept on, Lark let her head fall back and closed her eyes.

"You do realize it's only midnight."

The cushion beside her dipped as Keaton joined her on the couch. The substantial differences in their weight caused him to sink deeper into the cushions and Lark slipped toward the resulting dip, reducing the distance between them. She kept her eyes closed and let her other senses come alive.

"That's all?" she murmured, revived by the rhythm of her vigorous heartbeat.

His shoulder bumped against hers. He smelled like soap and baby powder from Grace's last change. "She's finally quiet."

The sleeve of his crisp cotton shirt grazed across

the top of her arms as he reached out to Grace. Sitting beside Keaton reminded Lark how long it had been since she'd let a man get close to her.

Although she'd had relationships in college and dated frequently the year she'd worked at Houston Methodist Hospital, since returning to Royal, Lark's love life had been limited to a few first dates with men she'd met online.

"But is she sleeping?"

"Not yet." His breath puffed against her temple.

She turned her head toward him and waited, wondering if he wanted to repeat their earlier kiss. When nothing happened, she opened her eyes. He was staring past her, gaze glued to a distant spot. Her lips parted as the longing for his kiss overwhelmed her. What would he do if she told him how she felt? Would he sweep her into his arms and drink deeply of her hunger or excuse the earlier kiss as a mistake?

Keaton withdrew his arm, and Lark's practical nature reasserted itself. What was she thinking? She couldn't get involved with Keaton. Look what had happened to Skye's relationship with their parents when the truth had come out about her and Jake. If anything happened between Lark and Keaton, there would be no running away. Keaton's life was the Holts' ranch, and Lark hadn't been happy living away from Royal. This was where she belonged. No, better that she and Keaton work together to take care of Grace and ignore whatever chemistry had sparked between them.

"You should move in." The blunt declaration came out of nowhere and surprised Lark as much as it did Keaton.

"Are you sure?"

"Absolutely. After tonight I can't imagine doing this alone."

"What about your parents? You know your father will object."

"Too bad." Annoyance smoldered in her gut. "If I can't count on their help, they lose the right to criticize what I do to ensure Grace's welfare."

"I'll bring my stuff by tomorrow. In the meantime, since this little lady is momentarily content, why don't you run off to bed and grab what sleep you can?"

"What about you?"

"Your couch is pretty comfortable. I'll just stretch out here."

"You're sure?" Lark was perfectly willing to keep him company. Perhaps too willing.

"Positive. Besides, you worked last night and no doubt are half-asleep already."

"Okay, just for a little while. When she wakes for her next feeding, get me up."

The road in front of Keaton's truck blurred for a moment, forcing him to give his head a fervent shake. A giant yawn followed. Three days of hard labor at the ranch. Three evenings of caring for Grace. Three nights plagued by the temptation of Lark sleeping a dozen strides away.

Damn. He was worn, frazzled and restless.

Grace's most difficult time of the day began as the sun went down. This was when she grew fussy and nothing they did seemed to satisfy her completely. That meant she didn't want to eat despite being hungry. Which meant she wasn't falling asleep after only half an hour of wakefulness. Tired and hungry, she grew more irritable by the second. And his inability to soothe her distress roused feelings of helplessness he'd never known before.

Lark wasn't faring much better. During the day Grace had decided she liked being held while she slept, so Lark wasn't free to take care of anything around the house. At first she resisted his suggestion that she needed a housekeeper to help, but on the third day after the laundry piled up and they'd eaten takeout three nights running, she'd caved to his insistence that she needed domestic assistance.

Once Jen had started working, things had gone more smoothly with the household chores, but keeping Grace content remained a challenge.

Keaton's respect for parents had grown during the last several days. He'd never imagined how much work went into taking care of a baby. It made a twelve-hour day in the saddle rounding up cattle seem like a ride on a merry-go-round.

If either of them had considered revisiting the kiss they'd shared that first night, it was lost in feedings, diapering, swaddling and soothing Grace. Maybe that was a good thing. The brief taste of her lips had been a mind-blowing surprise. Who would have guessed a simple kiss could ignite his senses? He'd been deaf and blind to everything but the incredible pliancy of her lips, the way her breath had caught, how she'd quivered at his touch.

Had he ever kissed a woman who'd responded to him with such genuine longing? It had stunned him. Left him wanting so much more. Keaton shifted his weight to ease the sudden heaviness in his loins. If just thinking about Lark aroused him, what would it be like to make love to her? Was it madness to consider it? Hadn't enough trouble been caused by Jake falling in love with Skye? And what made him think that Lark was willing to risk a similar rift with her parents? She was far more practical and cautious than her sister. Less willing to make waves.

Look at how she'd struggled with her decision to allow him to help her with Grace and permit him to move in. If she hadn't been desperate, he doubted she'd have accepted his assistance. She was far too worried about her father's reaction.

Arriving at Lark's house, Keaton fetched his latest purchase from the back of the pickup. It was a windup swing for Grace. His foreman had suggested it and Keaton had headed straight to the store. He hoped Grace would find it a suitable substitute for being held so Lark could get a break.

He noticed an eerie stillness to Lark's house the moment he entered. For a second, his heart stopped. Because her premature birth meant Grace's lungs hadn't fully developed, Lark intended to keep her home unless absolutely necessary. Had something happened while he was at the ranch? Setting the box inside the foyer, he advanced into the living room. The succulent scent of roast beef struck him the same instant he spied Lark sacked out on the couch, a sleeping Grace splayed across her chest.

The adorable picture held him transfixed. Keaton had never imagined himself living with, much less marrying a woman. Every one he'd dated had satisfied his physical desires or matched him intellectually, but he'd never found the right balance. In three short days Lark had demonstrated the perfect combination of physical allure and mental acumen.

Keaton retreated to the kitchen and snagged a beer from the refrigerator. Twisting off the top, he drained half the bottle. He was tired. Not thinking straight. Why else would he have settled on the daughter of his family's archenemy as his ideal match?

His gaze wandered back to Lark. Her right hand rested against Grace's side, blocking the infant from accidentally sliding off. Not that it could happen. Grace was as limp and unmoving as a rag doll.

Behind him, a timer went off. The noise caused Lark to stir. Her eyes opened. She blinked a few times, then caught sight of Keaton.

"How long have you been home?" Not *here*, but *home*, as if she'd come to accept that her house was his, as well. At least for the time being.

"A couple minutes. You were sleeping so peacefully I didn't want to wake you."

She rubbed her eyes with the back of her hand. "What time is it?"

"About five."

Lark was struggling to sit up without disturbing Grace. Keaton set his beer on the counter and went to take charge of the baby. She didn't wake as he transferred her to the crook of his arm.

"I know you feel more comfortable having Grace in your bedroom," he began, broaching a subject that was loaded with land mines. He offered his hand in aid. "But I think you need to consider moving her into the nursery."

"I like her sleeping in my room." She let him pull her to her feet, but freed herself as soon as she was upright. "Having her clear across the house is just too far."

"But I'll be right next door." He gazed down at the sleeping infant in his arms. Grace's rosebud mouth puckered as if she were nursing. It was adorable. "I'll have a monitor and I'm a light sleeper." Keaton watched Lark grapple with his request and decided not to allow her too much room to think. "I know it drives you crazy that I have to go into your bedroom every time Grace needs a change."

Her discomfort had been palpable the first night he'd officially moved in. She'd been twitchy throughout dinner and wouldn't let Keaton near Grace even though she'd seen how capable he was the night before.

"No, it's fine."

"Besides, there isn't enough space between the crib and the changing table. And there's no room for her clothes." Keaton had a hard time with the disorder. Things being out of place were his hot button. Jeb, his foreman, was used to it, but Keaton knew it drove a lot of the ranch hands crazy. "I'm going to bring someone in to paint the spare room a soft yellow. Grace isn't sleeping in the crib at the moment. Let's just move it and the changing table out of your room. Meanwhile she can continue to sleep in the bassinet."

Lark looked as if she wanted to argue, but Keaton knew what he'd suggested made perfect sense. First he would get the nursery set up. Later he could work on convincing her that Grace should spend some of her nights there so Lark could get a full night's sleep.

"Can we talk about this later," Lark murmured. "I have to finish getting dinner ready."

"It smells wonderful," he said, willing to drop the matter for the moment.

Keaton was happy enough that he'd spoken his piece. Even if Lark didn't agree to his plan, he'd already stated his intention and he would get the ball rolling.

"My friend Julie from the hospital went grocery shopping for me today and stuck around long enough for me to get the roast in. I couldn't stomach another takeout meal."

"Sounds great. Home-cooked meals have been rare for me since the tornado destroyed the ranch house."

She opened the oven door and checked on the status of the roast. "That's a lot of pressure to put on my cooking abilities."

"If it tastes half as good as it smells, I'll be happy."

She shot him a suspicious look but discovered he was completely serious and visibly relaxed. "Do you mind holding Grace for a little while? I also baked a cake this afternoon, but I haven't had a chance to frost it yet."

Grace began to stir. "Not at all. I think she might be in need of a change. I'll go take care of that."

Grace's furniture had been set up in what was supposed to be a small sitting area. The space was designed to hold a single chair and ottoman or a small writing desk. Keaton barely fit into the space between the changing table and the crib. The latter was being used to store diapers, clothes and toys that Grace would one day play with.

Below the crib were some of the items that Keaton had bought on his first shopping excursion. Lark had been so focused on Grace's immediate needs she hadn't gotten around to unpacking everything yet. As soon as he changed Grace, Keaton leaned down to poke through the bag. He recalled the saleslady had suggested a number of items in rapid-fire succession. Having no idea what they did or didn't need for a baby, he'd bought everything she suggested. Now he pulled out an infant gym and some sort of wrap.

With Grace tucked against his chest, he carried both items back to the living room. From the kitchen came the sound of humming. He glanced toward Lark. She was completely focused on smoothing white icing onto a triple-layer yellow cake. Her pleasure in the task made it hard for him to look away. Only when Grace began to squirm did he switch his attention.

Since opening and assembling the infant gym was going to be impossible one-handed, Keaton sat down on the floor, stretched out his legs and settled Grace on his lap. The new perspective engaged her interest, and when she started to fuss, he bent his knees and bounced her a little until she calmed.

Once he had the gym mat placed on the floor and the various toys attached to the padded tubes that crisscrossed over the baby, he slipped Grace inside the structure and held his breath. A newborn's ability to focus was limited to a range of twelve inches, but he wasn't sure how that applied to preemies. Grace had been born some thirteen weeks earlier, but her adjusted age was closer to three weeks.

The bright-colored animals dangling above Grace were a huge hit. She gurgled in delight as she reached up and batted at a monkey. It swung wildly and Grace kicked in response. Keaton didn't expect much of a reprieve, so he turned to the second item, the wrap. It was a long, infinity scarf that had been designed to snuggle the baby tight against the wearer, thus freeing the hands. For a baby like Grace, who didn't want to be put down, it should enable Lark a little more freedom.

But first he had to figure out how to make it work. Like the swaddling, the trick was to manage all the folds of the fabric. After watching a video on his tablet, he used one of Grace's stuffed animals for practice. The soft bunny was smaller than Grace, so he wasn't sure how secure the wrap would keep her, but it would be worth a try.

"What are you wearing?"

Keaton looked up from tucking the toy bunny into the wrap and met Lark's amused gaze. His heart jumped at her relaxed expression. The lines of tension had faded from around her mouth, and the frown lines had smoothed out on her forehead.

"It's a wrap for carrying a baby. I thought if you put Grace in it, you could free up your hands."

"That certainly would be nice. Can you show me how it works?"

"I'm still trying to figure that out. Maybe together we can get it to function properly."

Although Keaton hadn't started out with ulterior motives when he began fitting the wrap around Lark's slim body, he quickly discovered the activity gave him the perfect excuse to skim his fingers all over her slender form.

"And then you wrap it around this way." He settled the fabric into place, noticing the slight jump in her body as he accidentally grazed his knuckles against her breast. "You should have two pockets. Here and here."

"Looks like I do." She sounded a trifle breathless. "Now what?"

"Now we take Buster Bunny and put him on your shoulder." After watching the video four times, Keaton felt pretty confident in the steps. "Next we settle his legs into this pouch and pull up the fabric around him."

"That doesn't feel very secure."

"We're not done. This side comes up like this."

He rocked the edge of the fabric up her torso, across her breasts and the stuffed rabbit tucked against her chest. Although he was working hard to keep his touch neutral, the intimacy of their proximity and the slight tremble in her muscles were eating away at his better judgment.

"That feels better," she said. "What's this piece for?"

"I'm getting there."

"I'm sorry, I didn't mean to rush you."

"Are you always so impatient?" He hadn't meant to sound flirtatious, but there was a teasing edge that had slipped into his tone.

"I'm not usually impatient at all." She bit her lip in confusion. "Something about this is making me anxious." With her hands she indicated the fabric wrapped around her torso.

"Is it making you feel claustrophobic?"

"I'm not sure that's it."

"Are you sure you want to keep going? I could take it off you."

The sensual tension in the room escalated. Lark vibrated with it. Keaton's body hummed in matching harmony.

"Keaton." She whispered his name as his hands encircled her waist, palms gliding up her rib cage. "What are we doing?"

He dipped his head and grazed her lips with his. "Save your questions for later."

"Okay."

With a groan he claimed her lips. She came alive

in his arms, pushing up on her toes, tunneling her fingers into his hair. The bunny became trapped between them as he dragged his mouth over hers, tasting a hint of buttercream icing.

Her mouth was hot and sweet and welcoming and Keaton feasted on her lips like a man offered a gift from the gods. She matched his passion, held nothing in reserve. It was this openness that allowed Keaton to reel his wayward desires back in.

"That was crazy," she gasped as soon as he freed her mouth.

"Not crazy," he corrected, "wonderful." Keaton framed her face with his fingers and held her still so he could scrutinize her face. "If you cook like you kiss, I'm going to be in trouble."

"In trouble how?" Shadows were creeping into her eyes.

"I won't be able to stop myself from wanting more."

Color flooded her cheeks. She hooked her fingers around his hands and pulled them away from her skin. "I don't think you'll have to worry on either account."

"What makes you say that?"

"Because you've never struck me as a man who does anything that isn't good for him."

If that was her attempt at a warning, she was going

to have to be a whole lot clearer. "What about kissing you isn't good for me?"

She set her hands on her hips and regarded him incredulously. "Have you forgotten the bad blood between our families? It already forced Skye and Jake out of town. Can you imagine how bad it would be if we were caught?"

"So what are we supposed to do with these feelings between us?"

"What feelings? It's just a simple case of proximity lust. Nothing more."

Keaton studied her, wondering if that was what she truly believed, or if it was a way to let him off the hook. "Is proximity lust a scientific term or something you just made up?"

"It is what it is."

Five

Lark fled to the kitchen without removing the wrap, leaving Keaton to deal with Grace. She needed a second to regain her composure, and that wasn't going to happen if he offered to help her out of the yards of fabric.

She set about readying a bottle for Grace and plating the roast and potatoes for her and Keaton. Earlier she'd opened a bottle of red wine, but now she wasn't sure if drinking alcohol was a good idea after what had just happened between her and Keaton. The last thing she needed was for her guard to falter. Or had that ship already sailed?

"Why don't you eat while I feed Grace?" she offered, carrying both plates to the dining room. She'd set the table earlier and now wondered what she'd been thinking to bring out her crystal candleholders and best china.

"The table looks very nice, but you shouldn't have gone to so much trouble."

"No trouble." She relieved him of Grace and gestured toward a chair. "I opened a really nice Cabernet, or there's beer or whiskey." She was rambling because he was staring at her, his gaze inscrutable.

"The Cabernet sounds perfect. Let me get it. You sit and I'll get Grace's bottle too."

Lark dropped into her seat and discovered she still had the rabbit tucked into the wrap. With a wry grin, she plucked the stuffed animal free and shifted Grace's tiny form into the pouch. The baby's eyes widened as she settled into the sling, but Keaton had appeared with the bottle before Grace started to cry.

"I'm going to have to figure out the proper way to use this," Lark said, stabbing a piece of carrot with her left hand and lifting it to her mouth. "Being able to free up even one of my hands is really nice."

They traded off when Grace needed to be burped. Keaton had a knack for getting the infant to release the bit of air that she consumed with the formula. While he gently patted Grace's back, Lark quickly wolfed down her dinner. She hadn't realized how hungry she was until she popped the first bit of roast into her mouth.

"I don't think I ate lunch today," she remarked, shaking her head over her absentmindedness. "Grace was awake more than usual in the morning and then Julie came by and freed me up so I could get dinner ready. I don't know where the time goes."

"Babies take up more time than I imagined possible," Keaton agreed. "And I think establishing a routine with Grace will eventually help, but right now we're both learning about her needs and how best to meet them."

"Thanks."

"For what?"

"For saying exactly the right thing to stop me from feeling so overwhelmed. I just need to take it one day at a time."

"We," he corrected. "I'm here for Grace, as well. You don't have to do everything yourself."

Without warning, her chest tightened to the point of pain. Even though she'd let Keaton move in and surrendered part of Grace's care, she hadn't really let herself rely on him. In her mind he was an extra pair of hands that freed her up for short periods of time. Since bringing Grace home four days ago, she hadn't left the house, because to do so would be to fully relinquish responsibility for Grace to him, and Lark wasn't comfortable doing that.

"I haven't visited Skye since Grace left the hospital. Would you be okay if I went first thing tomorrow? I'll only be an hour or so."

"That's not a problem. I have the electrical inspection for the ranch house tomorrow, but it's not until the afternoon." Keaton reached across the table for Grace's bottle and settled her into his arm so he could finish feeding her. "Don't worry about us, we'll be just fine."

"Keaton moved in to help me with Grace," Lark told her sister after glancing around to make sure she couldn't be overheard. Her nerves were already a tangled mess. She didn't need the added stress of becoming the focus of hospital gossip. "The day we brought Grace home he suggested the idea and I should have turned him down flat. I mean, what was he thinking that I couldn't handle things?"

Hands moving compulsively across Skye's bed linens, smoothing, straightening, Lark let her thoughts revel in the previous night's kiss. It was what she really wanted to talk to Skye about, but she'd never been one to share something so private and needed to warm up to the telling.

"But then Grace had a bad first night. Oh, don't

worry. She didn't get sick or anything," Lark rushed to assure her sister. "But I think the transition from the NICU to my house was a little jarring. She couldn't calm down and then we had trouble swaddling her."

Of course, recalling that night revived the memory of that first, brief kiss and how soft Keaton's lips had been. Lark closed her eyes and swayed a little as she relived the delicious sensations she'd experienced.

"Apparently she likes being swaddled really tight." Lark noticed that she'd grabbed fistfuls of Skye's blanket, and released her grip with a soft exhalation of self-disgust. Was Julie's theory of proximity lust the best explanation for the way her body awakened to his slightest touch? "It took us quite a few tries to figure that out. And somewhere in the middle of all that, he kissed me."

Lark half expected her sister's eyes to fly open at such shocking news, but Skye remained unconscious. "It was a nice kiss. Impulsive. Didn't last long."

Spilling this first secret had taken its toll. Lark bustled around, checking the equipment in a feeble attempt to calm her pulse and restore normal breathing. When it became apparent that her emotions were messing with her body's electrical signals, Lark decided the best thing to do would be to spill everything all at once.

"He kissed me again a few days later. This one was longer and more premeditated. He made me feel as if I was the sexiest woman alive. Is that how Jake makes you feel?" She felt a little stupid asking. "Of course, that's why you left with him, isn't it? I've never had anyone treat me like that before. I wanted to…"

Confession might be good for the soul, but Lark had only just admitted to herself what she'd wanted that night. Her hormones, on alert since the night before, quickened. A mild ache invaded her body.

"Funny about Keaton," she continued. "I expected him to be the kind of guy who got in and got things done." Not exactly a flattering description, but he was always so stern and efficient. "How was I supposed to know he'd be so passionate? Such a great kisser. I…I didn't want him to stop."

There. She'd said it. The truth was out in the open. She wanted to have sex with Keaton Holt. Lark clapped her hands over her mouth and stared at Skye. Why wouldn't her sister wake up and give her advice about how to handle things with Keaton? She was completely out of her depth. No man had ever made her long to tear his clothes off and take big bites out of him. Well, not literally.

It was just the thought of both of them naked. His big body pinning her to the mattress. Or a wall. While he drove inside her…

Lark gave her head a vehement shake to clear it of such thoughts. She couldn't want those things with Keaton. He was a Holt. She was a Taylor. Her sister and Jake had left Royal in order to be together. The town was too small to hide a romantic relationship. Word would get out. Her parents would never forgive her.

Keaton was standing in the middle of Lark's empty third bedroom, slowly rocking Grace, when he heard the door to the garage open. In a couple days Lark would be going back to work and he was going to take over the baby's care. He wanted Grace in the bedroom next to his so he could handle her late night feedings.

"What in heaven's name is that?" Lark's normally soft voice, coming loud and clear from the living room, rang with shock and dismay.

Obviously she'd discovered his newest purchase. Keaton strode into the living room and found Lark staring at the sixty-inch flat-screen television that had been delivered this morning.

"A television," he responded. "Surely you've seen one before."

"That's a television?" She set her hands on her lush hips and faced him. "It takes up the whole wall."

"The better to watch the play-offs and not miss anything."

"Play-offs?"

"Football..."

Although he'd never considered himself much of a TV watcher, he hadn't realized how much he enjoyed unwinding after a long day with a beer and a sports channel until he couldn't. Granted, both Lark and Grace were plenty entertaining. He found a great deal of satisfaction in watching Grace sleep and Lark read. But after they went off to bed, he had far too many hours to keep his mind occupied and paperwork wasn't cutting it.

All too often, his thoughts strayed in the direction of Lark's bedroom. He contemplated if she slept in pajamas or nightgowns. Cotton or silk. She owned a queen-size bed and he liked picturing her in the middle of it, asleep on her side, her body curved, hands beneath her cheek. He doubted she snored, but it amused him to wonder if she did. Did she puff out her breath in little spurts? Maybe she drooled.

This last should have turned him off, but he found the image intriguing. In the short time he'd been living with her, he'd discovered she wasn't much of a morning person. Until she got a cup of coffee into her, she was downright grumpy. But at the same time her defenses were down and she was far more likely to smile. Naturally she reserved her happiest expressions for Grace, but what Lark didn't realize was that even though her grins weren't directed at him, he got to enjoy them, as well.

"It will only be here as long as I am," Keaton assured her. "Or until the ranch house is finished enough to receive it."

Lark gave the television the evil eye and then turned her back on it as if what she couldn't see didn't exist.

"It's getting late," she said. "Let me take Grace so you can get going."

Despite his need to be at a meeting at the Texas Cattleman's Club in thirty minutes, Keaton was reluctant to give up his niece. He'd enjoyed their time together. Since bringing her home, Lark had been Grace's primary caregiver, making Keaton feel like an unnecessary third wheel. Today, being alone and in charge, he'd been able to relax fully. Granted, Grace had slept through most of Lark's absence, but if she'd needed anything, he would have been ready and able to take care of it.

"The remote is on the coffee table," he said as

he handed Grace over. "If you want to check out the TV."

Lark wrinkled her nose. "Not really my thing."

"When I get home later, we can watch the Discovery Channel together. You might find that you like what you see."

"You are persistent, aren't you?"

"If by persistent you mean bullheaded, then yes." He'd hoped for a smile but had to settle for a sparkle in her moss-green eyes. "I won't be home until around eight tonight. I have a dinner meeting. Will you be okay?"

"We'll be fine."

Reluctant as always, Keaton headed out to his truck. As he backed down her driveway and pointed the vehicle in the direction of the Texas Cattleman's Club, he wondered why leaving her and Grace took so much effort. Although he'd shared the ranch house with his parents until the tornado wiped it out, the place was big enough that he didn't spend all that much time with them.

Basically he was accustomed to being alone.

But since moving into Lark's cozy house, sharing space with her and Grace, he'd adapted to their company. When Lark visited her sister in the hospital, her house had an empty feeling about it that nagged at him. He liked being with her. More than that, he craved her companionship.

It was an unexpected development for a lone wolf like him. Then he remembered that wolves were pack animals. Maybe he'd just been waiting for the right woman to come along. Was the change temporary? When he and Lark stopped playing temporary family, would all his longing for her dissipate? That he hoped it wouldn't trouble him.

She'd made it pretty clear that she didn't trust him. For years her parents had filled her head with inflammatory rhetoric against the Holt family. He might have overcome her reservations regarding his right to help with Grace, but despite the soul-stirring kisses they'd shared and her acknowledging a case of proximity lust, Keaton doubted she'd want to have anything to do with him once Skye and/or Jake claimed Grace.

Too bad she was such a tempting package. If he hadn't been driving, he might have shut his eyes to better savor the memory of her curves beneath his hands. Full breasts, narrow waist, flaring hips. Add to all that her long legs and the way she'd fit into his arms. Most men didn't notice her latent sensuality. She'd spent her entire life building a defense of invisibility.

It had never worked on Keaton. She'd always stood

out to him. A tranquil pool amidst the white-water rapids of the people around her. Her still waters ran deep and he found this endlessly fascinating.

Keaton put his mulling aside as he parked his truck beside the rambling single-story building that housed the Texas Cattleman's Club and strolled toward the clubhouse's front door. The interior decor was classic men's club. Dark paneling, lots of leather chairs and the walls were lined with hunting trophies.

A few years earlier the club had opened its doors to a few women. This had caused a great deal of consternation in many of its members. They'd grumbled and fussed, but the women had remained and then proceeded to ruffle even more feathers by transforming the billiards room into an on-site day care.

Keaton had sat back and watched the entire drama unfold, saying little, but throwing his support toward the women. It was long past time the Texas Cattleman's Club stepped into the twenty-first century. Watching Tyrone Taylor sputter in ineffectual annoyance had merely been a satisfying bonus.

The status update meeting had already begun when Keaton entered one of the private meeting rooms and took a seat in the back. President Gil Addison stood at the front of the room, running through the list of all the ongoing projects the members were in charge of.

"How are our tarp teams doing?" he asked Whit Daltry, owner of Daltry Property Management. His task had been to coordinate small groups of people to make sure damaged roofs were covered until repairs could be made.

"They were keeping up pretty well until the wind kicked up last week. At least we haven't had much rain."

A murmur of agreement went up around the room. Keaton nodded. He'd volunteered to coordinate the club's efforts to clean up the demolished town hall and preserve whatever records hadn't been damaged by the tornado. Much of the building's rubble had been cleared and they were close to being able to get at the filing cabinets. Depending on the ability of the old cabinets to withstand a building coming down on them, it was going to be dicey getting the records out intact. For the last few weeks he was wishing he'd volunteered to head up the chainsaw team.

When they finished the official business and Gil concluded the meeting, Keaton waved at a few of the other members, but didn't linger to chat with anyone. The meeting had run longer than he'd expected and he was late for an appointment with the acting mayor to discuss his concerns about moving the town's records.

As he drove, his phone chimed and the truck's electronic voice announced that he'd received a text from Lark. He listened as the message was read to him and then smiled. She'd sent him another of those artistic pictures of blissfully sleeping Grace dressed like a fairy amongst flowers or sailing in a boat. Lark used fabric to create the scene on the floor and then set Grace into the tableau.

At a stop sign, he checked the photo she'd sent him and chuckled at the sight of Grace as Rapunzel in her tower. Lark's creativity surprised him over and over. If she wasn't baking and decorating cakes, she was seeking other outlets for her rich imagination.

Suddenly he was glad she'd spent her entire life building a defense of invisibility. If she'd let more people see who she really was, she might have gotten married before Keaton wised up.

But despite the soul-stirring kisses they'd shared and her acknowledging a case of proximity lust, Keaton wasn't sure she wanted him to stick around once Skye and/or Jake claimed Grace.

And not for the first time that uncertainty was accompanied by a heaviness in his chest and a weighty sense of dread.

* * *

Lark felt sluggish and dull as she left her car parked in the hospital's employee lot and leaned into the chilly January wind on her way to the entrance. Grace had developed a case of the hiccups after her four o'clock feeding, and Lark hadn't been able to get her back to sleep until almost six. By then it was only an hour until she had to get ready for work, so she'd decided to bake a batch of cinnamon rolls to share with her fellow nurses since Marsha wasn't on duty and couldn't complain about the treat.

It was her first day back since bringing Grace home, and already Lark could feel anxiety getting the better of her. Keaton would be annoyed if he suspected how she was feeling. They'd had several tense conversations regarding her reluctance to let him be fully in control. Well, today she didn't have much choice.

Lark swung by the surgical floor to drop off half the cinnamon rolls for her former coworkers. Even if her stint in the ICU hadn't been difficult and lonely, she would have missed the camaraderie she shared with Julie, Yvonne, Hazel and Penny. They were smart, hardworking women who functioned like a team and had little interest in hospital gossip.

Julie was in her office when Lark stopped by. Although she hadn't known the pretty brunette more than a couple months, Lark felt a real connection with her. Born in South Africa, Julie had traveled extensively around the world before coming to Royal to work with Dr. Lucas Wakefield, the brilliant surgeon who'd saved Skye and Grace.

"I brought treats," Lark announced, setting the pan of rolls on Julie's desk.

"Isn't that just like you to think about everyone but yourself? You look half-dead on your feet." Julie's brown eyes narrowed in concern. "How are things going with Grace?"

"Better, but it's something new every day. Last night she had the hiccups."

"Oh dear." Julie popped the lid on the rolls and inhaled deeply. "They're still warm. How did you find time to bake?"

Lark covered a yawn with one hand while waving away Julie's concern with the other. "I had a free hour this morning."

"You are amazing. How is living with Keaton going?"

"Fine. We had the talk."

"The one where you told him nothing was going to happen between you two?"

Lark thought back a few days. Had she spelled it out that succinctly? "I'm not sure. I told him your theory of proximity lust." She paused. Had she actually said there would be no more kissing? "I know I mentioned how bad it would be if we were caught…" She trailed off.

"But you didn't actually tell him to keep his lips to himself."

"I don't think I did."

"Because you don't want him to?"

"I guess." Was it lack of sleep that was making her ambivalent or something else? "I mean, no."

"You're not sounding very clear." Julie grinned at her. "I think you like him and are afraid of the repercussions because of what happened with your sister."

"I do like him. He's intelligent and a huge help with Grace. He's been a strong advocate for his brother even though none of us understand why Jake hasn't been in contact."

"Not to mention he's incredibly sexy in an intense, silent way."

Goose bumps rose on Lark's skin as she recalled the heat of his kiss and the way he'd watched her afterward. "He's tall. I actually have to look up at him."

"And he's built like he could wrestle calves all day and never break a sweat."

Lark laughed. "What do you know about wrestling calves?"

"Only what I've seen on TV, but it's enough to know you need to be tough."

"Okay, he's definitely on the rugged side and that's very appealing, but I would be crazy to think of him as anything but the one man in Royal that my father would never forgive me for getting involved with."

"Except that you're already involved with him. He's living in your house."

"To help me take care of Grace." Lark cringed when she thought of her father's inevitable reaction when he found out. "It would be so much worse if he thought we were sleeping together."

"So you're just going to ignore the chemistry between you?"

"That's the plan."

"Good luck."

Waving goodbye to Julie, Lark headed toward the ICU. Her nerves were a tangled mess. She'd been gone from the house, leaving Keaton in charge for a whopping half hour, and already she wanted badly to call and see how things were going. What bothered her was that only part of her wanted an update on Grace; she mainly desired contact with Keaton. He'd gotten under her skin in a very short period of time.

As a compromise between instinct and logic, she

sent him a text instead of calling. This way she satisfied her need to connect with him but maintained her distance. It was going to be a balancing act until she got her emotions under control. It would be hard—living in close proximity, desiring his hands against her skin, quelling the urge to press her body against his while maintaining a casual, unaffected demeanor. Lark shuddered in dismay.

The ICU nurses' station was slammed when Lark arrived. Apparently Marsha had gone home with a headache halfway through her shift and one of the surgical patients who had undergone a routine knee replacement had developed a blood clot that had moved into his lungs.

This meant Lark wouldn't have the opportunity to ease back into her job and wouldn't have more than five minutes to stop by Skye's bedside. With time running short before her shift started, Lark pulled out her phone for one last thing. She set it on Skye's chest, right over her sister's heart, and hit the play button.

"I brought you a video of Grace doing this weird grunting thing that is typical of preemies. She's lying in the infant gym that Keaton bought her and playing with the monkey. It's her favorite animal. I know you can't watch her yet, but I hope her voice reaches you." Lark started the video and watched

Skye's face for some reaction. She had no idea if her sister was aware but if anything could reach a new mother, it was adorable baby noises, and Grace made more of those each day.

"Keaton bought a sixty-inch flat-screen and put it in my great room," Lark complained, cuing up the video to play again. "Apparently he can't live without football. The thing is monstrous. He insisted we watch a show on the Discovery Channel. It was interesting, but the programing on the History Channel was more to my taste. And then there's this show about women in search of the perfect wedding dress." Lark had found that one on her own. The gorgeous wedding dresses had left her contemplating what sort of bridal gown Skye would choose.

Lark surveyed her sister's bare hand. Surely when she'd gotten pregnant, Jake would have proposed. He'd want to make sure Grace had his name. Lark shied away from considering that Keaton's brother wasn't the honorable sort. Had Skye been the one who'd balked? Why, when she'd adored Jake for so long?

After she'd connected with her sister, the rest of Lark's day bordered on frantic. At least being busy kept her from worrying how Grace and Keaton were doing. Halfway through her shift, she was able to take a twenty-minute break to grab lunch and check her messages. Her inbox was filled with pictures of Grace sleeping peacefully in her bassinet or the mechanical swing Keaton had bought. Her relief was instantaneous. Why had she worried? Grace was in good hands.

Six

Keaton kept his ear tuned to the swing in the living room where Grace slept while he checked out the job the painters had done on what would become the nursery. He'd bought odorless paint, but until it was completely dry and the fumes had cleared, he didn't want Grace in here.

He hoped Lark would be pleasantly surprised. After seeing her weariness this morning, he'd determined the best thing for her would be moving Grace into her own room so Lark could sleep through the nights she had to work the following day.

"Looks great," he told the artist he'd hired to decorate the newly painted walls with images plucked from the crib bedding.

"Thanks." Tracey had placed a monkey above where the changing table would go and a smattering of jungle creatures on the wall opposite the crib. "I hope your wife likes it."

Keaton didn't correct her. To explain the complicated relationship between him and Lark would take too much of his energy. Better that he say nothing. "Monkeys are Grace's favorite, so I'm sure Lark will approve."

Although Lark hadn't been overjoyed that Keaton had hired painters, her scowl carried less punch than when he'd first brought up the idea of hiring Jen to clean house and prepare meals a couple times a week. He'd wanted her full-time, but Lark refused. She hadn't quite given up her determination to do more than was physically possible, but Keaton had his own streak of stubbornness. Grace needed her aunt to be in tiptop shape, and Lark needed to be at full strength to support Skye. He intended to do whatever necessary to see that she was.

From the living room, his satellite phone beeped, announcing a call. Cell coverage had been disrupted at the ranch since the tornado damaged the equipment on the nearby tower. Keaton had picked up a couple satellite phones that he and the foreman used to keep in touch with the various contractors they had working on repairs.

Grace slept peacefully despite the phone ringing nearby, but Keaton decided to take the call in the kitchen. It was close to her feeding time, so he might as well get a bottle ready.

"Keaton, how are you?" His mother sounded relaxed and happy. "How are things at the ranch?"

"Fine, Mom. Everything's fine. How are you and Dad?" His parents were shopping for retirement property on the Alabama gulf coast.

"We're enjoying the beach, but your father is frustrated with the real estate market here." His mother sounded amused. With Keaton in charge of the family ranch, David Holt had been free to throw his abundant energy into finding his wife the perfect home.

"Sorry to hear that."

"And I think he's anxious about the ranch. So we're coming home in a few days."

"I hope he's not disappointed with the progress."

"Do you think Lark would mind if we came over there and spent time with Grace when we get back to town?"

Keaton was pleased his mother no longer sounded suspicious when she spoke of Lark. Initially his parents had had a very negative reaction to his announcement that he was moving into Lark's house, but they trusted his judgment and he'd plied them with stories of Lark's earnestness and devotion to her sister and Baby Grace until they'd come around.

"I think she'd be glad to have you. Let me check with her when she comes home tonight."

In truth, he wasn't sure how Lark would react to his mother's request. She'd yet to receive an answer to the invitation she'd extended to her parents despite having called twice since Grace had come home from the hospital. The lack of contact agitated her. Keaton hated seeing her distress. As angry as his parents had been when they found out that Jake had been secretly seeing Skye through high school and college, as the years had gone by without contact with their son, their attitude toward Skye and, by extension, the rest of the Taylors had mellowed.

If only the Taylors felt the same way.

"I'll give you a call later tonight and let you know what Lark says," he told his mother before ending the call.

No more than five minutes later Grace began to fuss. Pleased that he was developing a sixth sense where she was concerned, Keaton headed for the swing before she had a chance to let out her first wail.

Lark let herself into the kitchen and pushed the button that would close the garage door. All the way home she'd been dreading what sort of chaotic mess she'd find her house in. To her delight, there were a neat row of drying bottles lined up on the countertop and a delicious smell wafting from the oven. Soothing music poured from her stereo speakers. Keaton had found her collection of interpretive piano CDs.

Before she shrugged out of her coat, Keaton appeared at her side with a glass of white wine. "Dinner will be ready in twenty minutes if you want to grab a quick shower."

"You did all this?"

"I had a very smooth day with Grace. That left me with enough free time to stay caught up." He took her coat and handed her the wine. "How was your first day back?"

"Awful." She sipped the wine and sighed. "Is there really time for me to take a shower?" The thought of letting hot water wash away her stressful day sounded blissfully perfect.

"There's time." He gave her a little shove in the direction of her bedroom. "Just don't fall asleep in there."

Drifting in a fog of pleasure, Lark sipped her wine and peeled off her scrubs. Leaving them in a pile on her bathroom floor, she started the water running in her shower and blinked to restore moisture to her dry eyes. The last twelve hours were beginning to feel like a bad dream. She took another sip of wine and felt the knots in her shoulders begin to unravel. She'd never imagined how wonderful it would be to have a family to come home to after a long day.

Ten minutes later, wrapped in a thick terry robe, her hair still damp, Lark reentered her bedroom and stopped when she realized Grace's crib and changing table were no longer in the little sitting area. She and Keaton had talked about moving Grace into the third bedroom, but Lark wasn't ready to have the baby so far away. Instead of respecting her decision, he'd gone ahead and done what he believed was best.

Lark stalked out of her bedroom and headed for the kitchen, where Keaton was sliding a cookie sheet covered with dinner rolls into the oven. "I thought you understood that I wasn't ready to have Grace move."

Keaton closed the oven door and turned to face her. His eyebrows drew together as he took in her damp hair, robe and bare feet.

"Grace will be fine in her own room. You need to be able to sleep the nights you work, and this way I have freer access."

His calm explanation had the opposite effect on Lark. "This is my house," she reminded him, her temper flaring. "I should be the one who decides what happens here. You've already insisted on hiring a housekeeper and brought in a huge TV. Now you've moved Grace."

"Look, it's going to be okay." He took her upper arms in a strong grip and gave her a little shake. "You just need to let me help."

All the fight went out of Lark as her body became immediately aroused by Keaton's touch. Despite the thickness of the terry cloth, Lark could feel his heat. It flowed into her in a rush, igniting the desire she'd worked so hard these past few days to ignore.

"Keaton." Her voice cracked on his name. She had no idea how to verbalize what she needed. Her skin longed for the imprint of his hands. The ache between her thighs flared, demanding relief from the endless hours of anticipation. Her instincts took over. "Kiss me."

His body stiffened at her plea…demand…whatever it had been. Concerned that she'd been too bold and embarrassed by his inaction, she was on the verge of explaining that she'd been kidding when he growled.

"Damn it, Lark." His lips dipped toward hers but hovered before he made contact.

"What are you waiting for?"

His grip on her arms tightened. The corner of

his mouth jerked. "You Taylor girls are nothing but trouble."

Stung, she pulled back. Keaton's long fingers held her prisoner. "What's that supposed to mean?"

"Just what I said. You're trouble."

"I'm not the one who demanded we share responsibility for Grace or suggested you move in. That's all on you."

His fingers refused to relax their grip and she couldn't risk struggling to free herself or he would get an eyeful of her bare form. As if he read her thoughts, Keaton's gaze raked down her body.

"You have gorgeous breasts," he murmured. "Why do you insist on hiding them?"

The awe in his voice was such a contrast to his annoyance a moment earlier that Lark was at a loss. "How do you know what my breasts look like?"

"There's a great lake for swimming on the edge of Taylor land. When it was hot, you used to ride there and go swimming on the days you weren't working at the mall."

As soon as Lark had been old enough to get a part-time job, she started working a minimum of twenty hours a week. The income allowed her to buy her first car and limited the amount of time she was at home, enduring her mother's nonstop criticism.

"How did you know that?" Then she realized what he hadn't said. "You watched me?"

"Are you kidding? I was a horny college student and you wore a tiny yellow bikini."

Her skin burned as she thought back to those days. Believing herself alone, she'd shed her inhibitions and reveled in being sensual and free.

"But that was my family's land."

"And it pissed me off that you had the best swimming hole for miles around. So I trespassed." His lips twisted into a humorless smile. "A lot."

"Why didn't you ever tell me you were there?"

"Because as long as you thought you were alone, you were like some wild water nymph. If you'd had any idea I was there, you'd have chased me off with that shotgun you always carried with you."

"I needed it to keep the predators at bay," she replied. "Looks like it worked."

"Now that you understand that I've been crazy about your beautiful body for a long time, will you please go get dressed." Keaton gently shoved her an arm's length away and set her free. "And hurry. Dinner will be ready in five minutes."

Knowing it would be supremely reckless to bait him further, Lark retreated. To her dismay, her knees had developed a perilous wobble and she had to sit on her bed for two minutes before she felt steady enough to dress. Slipping into jeans and a bulky sweater, she returned to the kitchen in time to help Keaton dish up the meal.

"This looks amazing," she said, hoping some mundane conversation would disperse the last bit of tension between them. "What is it?"

"Chicken covered in mayo and shredded Parmesan cheese. I saw the recipe on a commercial and it seemed easy enough."

"You are a man of many surprises," she murmured, carrying their plates to the dining room. Glancing over to where Grace slept in her swing, Lark realized the chance of distractions during the meal was low. She sat down and smiled up at Keaton as he topped off her wineglass. "You know, I think I've used this dining table more since you moved in than in the two years I've owned the house."

"Where do you usually eat?"

"At the breakfast bar." She smoothed her napkin across her lap, avoiding looking at Keaton.

Tonight he'd substituted a long-sleeve Henley in dark gray for his usual cotton button-downs. The knit material clung to his wide shoulders and highlighted his sculpted chest muscles. Heat flooded her cheeks as she recalled the solid wall of his torso pressed against her the last time they'd kissed. A five-foot-ten-inch girl with substantial curves would be crazy not to swoon over a man who was strong enough to manhandle her and smart enough to know when she wanted him to and when she didn't.

So far Keaton was that guy. He'd demonstrated both passion and restraint. If only his last name wasn't Holt.

"My mother called tonight. She and my dad are coming back to town in a few days," Keaton began, appearing oblivious of her musing.

What a relief. Usually he demonstrated an unsettling ability to read her thoughts and anticipate her needs.

"That's nice."

"Mom wondered if they could come over and spend some time with Grace. I thought maybe a family dinner?"

The word *family* gave her a jolt. Did he want her there? Or would he choose a night when she was working?

"Sure."

"You're off Wednesday, right?"

"I am." The strength of her relief speared through Lark, shocking her. "That should work great."

"And I don't want you to worry about dinner. I thought we'd fix steaks and keep things simple."

"I don't own a barbecue," Lark reminded him.

"That's okay. I've got it taken care of."

Taken care of how?

"Having your parents over for dinner is a great idea," she said. "They deserve to get to know their granddaughter." If only her parents were so inclined. "And thank you for asking me."

He didn't look at all chastened by her subtle reproof.

"Of course. It's your house."

He had to be kidding. Irritation flared. "That hasn't slowed you down thus far."

"I know I should have told you my plans for fixing up Grace's nursery," he said, returning to the disagreement they'd been having earlier. "But see it from my perspective. When Grace sleeps in your bedroom, I'm not able to do my fair share." He lowered his lids to half-mast and peered at her from beneath his lush lashes. "Unless, of course, you want me in your bedroom late at night."

She couldn't restrain the grin that tugged at her lips. "Stop trying to distract me from being annoyed with you."

"I'm not trying to distract you, I'm simply pointing out the reality of our current situation." Keaton rested his forearms on the table and leaned forward, his expression earnest. "I'm not going to pretend I understand what you're going through. With Skye in a coma and Grace's health a constant concern, you've got to be consumed with anxiety. All I'm trying to do is take some of the burden off your shoulders. Let me help."

Lark drew a shaky breath. With her stomach in knots she'd lost her appetite. "It's just so hard to let go. I keep worrying that she'll need me and I won't be there."

"Remember that she was on her own in the NICU for the first twelve weeks of her life."

"I know, but that makes me all the more determined to keep her close."

"And I'll be right next door with the baby monitor on my nightstand."

She knit her fingers together in her lap and struggled to overcome her compulsion to control every aspect of Grace's well-being. "Let's start tomorrow. Give me the night to get used to the idea."

Keaton nodded. "That sounds good."

"And if she hates being all by herself, we go back to what we've been doing."

"With one difference." Keaton picked up his fork and speared a broccoli floret. "I will be visiting your bedroom every two or three hours throughout the night."

Keaton lay on the bed in Lark's guest room, his hands behind his head, his feet crossed at the ankle, and stared at the dark ceiling. Even though it was Lark's night to get up with Grace, he couldn't sleep. Over the last few days he'd grown accustomed to his niece's schedule and woken every few hours just as she was beginning to stir. He glanced at the clock and decided to get up and get a bottle started. Maybe if he could catch Grace before she made a sound, he could give Lark a few more hours to rest.

For a man who spent his days directing the operations of an extensive ranch and getting dirty on occasion working alongside his hands, he was rather surprised how well he'd managed with Grace. Everything about her was so tiny it had taken him forever to master slipping on her doll-sized socks and days before he was completely confident in his ability to change her diaper and dress her without worrying that he might accidentally be too rough with her.

Each time she focused her gaze on his face, his heart took a severe hit for his absent brother. Jake was missing so much. And then there was Skye, still locked in a coma. There were so many firsts they both were missing.

Right on cue, Grace was beginning to wake up when he entered the nursery. He immediately turned down the baby monitor so if she did make a sound, Lark wouldn't hear. Pleased with his timing, Keaton lifted the infant into his arms and settled into the rocking chair he'd bought. As soon as he brought the bottle to her lips, Grace latched on and began sucking with enthusiasm.

"Hungry little thing, aren't you?"

It pleased him how the baby was thriving. Tomorrow was her first wellness check since leaving the hospital. He and Lark had agreed to go together, and if all went well, they were going to attempt an early dinner out. That should start the tongue-wagging, he thought, remembering how getting caught having dinner together had led to Jake and Skye running away from Royal. But then, they'd been in love. He and Lark were simply co-babysitting.

Yet if that was all it was, why did his thoughts circle back to her all day and much of the night? Getting up to feed or change Grace hadn't been much of a hardship since his sleep was all messed up by the temptation of her sleeping twenty feet away. Nor could he get out of his head the night she'd picked a fight over the nursery while wearing nothing more than a robe. Did she have any idea how close she'd come to driving him over the edge?

By the time Keaton resettled Grace in her crib and watched her fall asleep, his own exhaustion had caught up with him. But he knew it was nothing compared to how Lark must be feeling.

"Is something wrong with Grace?" Lark's soft voice, tense and filled with concern, came from the doorway behind him.

"She's fine," he reassured her, pitching his volume equally low. Turning his head in her direction, he caught her staring at him in dismay. What would it take for her to stop worrying so much?

"Why are you up, then?"

"I was awake and figured you could use the sleep." Since she seemed to be unable to shake her doubts, he held out his hand and beckoned her close. "She's all right, really."

Once she'd seen for herself that Grace was sleeping peacefully, Lark heaved a huge sigh. Then her attention shifted to him and her gaze sharpened.

"You aren't wearing a shirt."

He glanced down at his bare chest, unsure what to make of the accusation in her voice. "I don't usually wear one to bed."

"But you're not in bed."

"Obviously."

Since she seemed determined to pursue the odd conversation, he decided they'd be better off having it where they wouldn't disturb Grace. Taking Lark by the arm, he escorted her out of the nursery and deposited her stiff form in the middle of the living room.

"I've got everything under control. Go back to bed."

"It's my night to take care of her." Her lower lip jutted out, making her look like an adorable toddler in a temper.

Keaton set his hands on his hips above the waistband of his pajama bottoms, and struggled not to grin at how cute she looked. "I promise to sleep as soundly as a hibernating bear tomorrow. Now go to bed."

"Damn it, Keaton, you can't tell me what to do." She was in a transfixed stupor, staring at his half-naked form.

Again he glanced down at himself, wondering what she found so utterly fascinating. Then he looked at her.

Lark wore pale blue, long-sleeve pajamas that covered her from neck to ankle. Modest in fit, they still managed to accent the provocative swell of her substantial breasts and failed to hide the tightening of her nipples against the soft fabric.

His body came to life with such ferocity he almost groaned. "You should listen to me when I'm giving you good advice," he growled, unsure how much longer he could keep his hands off her.

She tipped her head back and met his gaze. Her

eyes were clear, the look in them bold. "What makes your advice so great?"

"It will keep me from doing something that won't make you very happy."

Her eyebrows rose. "Like what?"

Sexual tension flared between them at her defiant tone.

"Like this." Plagued by too many long nights of temptation and incensed that she'd dared him to act, Keaton seized the edges of her pajama top and tore it open. Buttons flew in all directions. Shocked by the ferocity of the desire she aroused in him, Keaton froze.

They were both breathing hard, but the ragged rise and fall of their chests was the only movement. Keaton searched Lark's stunned expression and waited for her to speak, to yell at him for stepping across the line.

Her hand came up, but not to slap him. She slid her palm up his chest, the caress brimming with sensual intent, and tunneled her fingers into his hair. Rising on tiptoe, she pressed her bare breasts against his chest and slid her cheek against his.

"Kiss me."

His lips were halfway to hers when she spoke the words.

This was no tentative, exploratory kiss. Lark's

mouth was open and eager as he claimed it. He wasted no energy on preliminaries, just plunged his tongue deep, and was rewarded by the ardent thrust of her pelvis against his growing erection. Her moan made his head spin.

Leaving one hand to cup her head, he let the other skim down her back. He savored every curve and dip as her skin slipped like silk beneath his questing fingers. When he reached the waistband of her pajama bottoms, he hesitated only briefly before diving beneath. The fullness of her butt was a temptation he could no longer resist. They groaned in unison as he filled his palm with her flesh, fitting her more firmly against his raging hardness.

If he didn't get her naked soon, he was going to descend into madness. Or perhaps he'd already plunged down the rabbit hole. He was fast losing track of which way was up, and when Lark stroked him through the cotton fabric covering his erection, he shuddered. She touched him with more curiosity than eroticism, but the contact was earth-shattering. With only a matter of moments before he could no longer stand, he eased down on one knee. Bracketing her lush hips between his hands to hold her still, he placed his lips against her flat stomach between her rib cage and belly button.

She quivered as he kissed a path across her abdomen and smoothed her hand across his shoulders. He needed a moment to gather himself for what came next. At long last, confident that he was ready, Keaton set his forehead against her body and spoke.

"If you go back to bed right now, we can both pretend that this was nothing more than an incredibly realistic dream."

Fabric whispered through the air as it fell to the floor. Seconds later Lark guided his hands up her body. Understanding what she wanted, he cupped her breasts, marveling at their perfection. The hardness of her nipples fascinated him. Her breath caught as he gave them a light pinch. She was so incredibly sensitive. He couldn't wait to make her body sing.

Eager to begin, Keaton lowered her to the carpet unable to make the long trek to her bedroom. As soon as her back met the floor, he moved over her, capturing her lips in a slow, drugging kiss. Her hands moved down his back, nails digging in, as he released her mouth to suck gently at the spot where her neck and shoulder met.

Beneath him her hips shifted restlessly, inciting his passion with each thrust against his overly stimulated flesh. Breathless, he licked his way down her chest and sucked her nipple into his mouth, distracting her momentarily. He brought his hand up to knead her other breast, and a soft mewling sound broke from her lips. Smiling, he used tongue and teeth to keep her attention fixed where he wanted it, but he underestimated her—she wasn't willing to be a passive participant.

Before he knew what she was up to, she'd spread her legs and tugged the waistband of his pajamas down past his hips. In an instant he was pressed against the heat between her thighs, the only barrier between them her pajama bottoms.

She slid her hand between their bodies and found him. The sensation of her bare skin on his hot shaft was too much for his willpower to bear. Keaton slid down her body, breaking contact. He trembled in the aftermath of what could have been a very quick end to their foreplay and trailed his mouth across her stomach. She lifted her hips to aid him in stripping her bare and he smiled as his lips dipped into the hollow near her hip. With her pants no longer in his way, he shifted his shoulders between her knees and gathered her butt in his hands.

"Keaton?"

It was all she managed before he put his mouth against her hot, sweet center.

Seven

With his tongue trailing fire around and over the most sensitive part of her body, Lark arched her back and quaked with pleasure unlike any she'd ever known. Keaton's mastery stole her voice and rendered her muscles useless. Her entire world became his mouth and the rapid building of pressure centered between her thighs.

He seemed to understand exactly what drove her wild. His touch was both clever and commanding. She rose higher and higher. An unbridled moan grew in her throat, the rumble vibrating through her as her orgasm built. It was crazy how fast and hard she was coming. She tried to slow it down, to linger in the moment, but Keaton slid two fingers inside her and touched a spot that sent her off like a rocket.

Blind and deaf, she shook with the intensity of her climax. For several heartbeats time stopped and she floated. Then she crashed back into her body and gasped.

"That was amazing."

Keaton kissed her stomach. "Glad you enjoyed it."

He lay between her thighs, with most of his weight supported on his arms, and watched her through heavy-lidded eyes, a half smile on his gorgeous lips.

"You look awfully pleased with yourself."

"Any time a man can get a woman to come like that, he has a right to feel smug."

"Is that so?" Before he guessed her intention, Lark wrapped her thighs around his waist and used the element of surprise to knock him off balance.

With Keaton flat on his back, she took a second to appreciate the width of his chest and all the fine muscles that made up the ridges of his abdomen. She drew her fingers over his collarbone and across his pecs to the flat disks of his nipples. He shuddered as she scraped her nails over them and with that her confidence ballooned.

Behind her, Keaton's erection bumped against her lower back. She reached for it and watched his eyes widen as she cupped him lightly. Immediately a familiar hum began below her belly button. She rocked her hips in a gentle arc. The motion stirred her body back to wakefulness, making her smile.

"What are you thinking about?" Keaton asked, cupping her breasts in firm fingers.

Lark pushed into his touch and gripped him more firmly. "I'm thinking that I've never been with anyone that makes me feel the way you do."

"And what way is that?"

"Like I'm hungry all the time. When I'm in the same room with you, all I can think about is this." She moved her fingers in provocative swirls, and Keaton's face screwed up as if in pain. "How it would feel to have you inside me."

She leaned forward and kissed him sweetly on the mouth. Her tongue licked along the seam of his lips, tasting the lingering flavor of her arousal, and when he parted for her, it dipped in to tease and tantalize.

When Keaton cupped her face and deepened the kiss, she let him. Her hunger spiked, driven to new heights by the passionate bite of Keaton's fingers and the ferocity of his kiss. Soon she knew she needed him to fill her. She broke free of Keaton's mouth and gasped in a great lungful of air. At the same time she shifted so the tip of his erection nudged at her, eager for what she offered.

With a sharp curse Keaton caught her hips in a firm grip. "Wait. We need protection."

She shook her head. "It's okay."

"Are you on something?"

"No, but I'm at a safe point in my cycle." She pried his hands off her and with a whooshing exhale, took him in.

An exclamation of surprise burst from her. She'd known he was big, but she wasn't prepared for the reality of how completely he filled her. "Wow."

"Are you okay?"

"I'm good."

He didn't look convinced. "You have a funny look on your face."

"I'm just getting used to all of you."

"Take your time." He caressed her thighs with a casualness that belied the tightness around his mouth, but when she started gyrating her hips, he sprang into action.

Before her mind recognized movement, Keaton rolled her beneath him and captured her lips in a sizzling kiss. At the same time he shifted his hips back and thrust slowly into her. The friction was amazing and Lark wrapped her legs around Keaton's hips as his rhythm built.

As they moved together she noticed that his earlier intensity had been tempered. He made love to her with deliberate concern for her needs. As much as she appreciated his thoughtfulness, she didn't like that he was holding back. She liked the wildness he aroused in her. It unleashed a sense of freedom missing in her life.

She bit down on his shoulder and dug her fingernails into his back. "Stop being so gentle," she growled when he stared down at her in confusion. "I'm not going to break. Give me all you've got."

"Fine." After uttering that single word, he kissed her hard and drove into her powerfully.

Lark grabbed handfuls of his hair and let her tongue duel with his. His need surrounded her, filled all the lonely places she'd gotten so good at ignoring. This was what it felt like to be truly wanted. No one had ever made love to her with such determination.

"Yes, yes, yes," she chanted when he let her breathe. "More, just like that."

An orgasm was rushing forward to claim her. Words poured from her. She heard them in her ears but could make no sense of the flow. They seemed to have an effect on Keaton, however, because he began to pound harder into her. Lark pried her eyes open and watched his face, sensing that he was close and wanting to see him come.

As a cry broke from his lips, the first shudders of

her own climax claimed her. His body jerked, his lips pulled back in a savage grin. He looked down, caught her gaze with his and held her captive as they exploded together.

"That was not appropriate," Keaton muttered, shifting his weight off Lark. His chest rose and fell in exaggerated breaths as he sat up and stared down at her.

She punched him in the shoulder. "The postcoital words every woman wants to hear."

The hit barely hurt, but it was enough to make her point. She might not expect flowery, romantic phrases, but she wasn't interested in stark realism either.

"I meant not using protection."

"I figured, but we'd already covered that issue before it happened. I told you it was not going to be a problem."

He raked his fingers through his hair, disturbed by what he'd done. "I don't have unprotected sex." He was furious with himself for the lapse.

"That's good to know." Heedless of her nakedness, she pushed to her feet and snatched her pajamas from the floor. "I don't either. I'm sorry if I made you do something so out of character."

She was halfway to her bedroom before he realized she'd misread the target of his irritation. By the time he leaped to his feet to pursue Lark and apologize, she was in the process of shutting her door firmly in his face. Ignoring the blatant "get lost" signal, he knocked.

And knocked again.

"Look," he called. "We need to talk about what happened."

The door muffled her voice, but her words were clear. "No, we don't."

"What just happened between us caught me off guard and I put my foot in it."

"You put your entire leg into it." She sounded closer, but no less annoyed.

"Open the door and I'll do better."

"I don't believe you can."

"No one has ever made me lose control the way you just did."

A long pause followed his words. "I'm listening."

"The reason I didn't insist on protection was that I couldn't stop. Never have I done something like that before. I couldn't bear to have anything come between us. But it was stupid and put you at risk."

The door cracked open. Lark peered at him through the narrow space. "Never?"

"Not once."

"You didn't put me at risk." She gave him a small smile. "But thanks for your concern."

And to his astonishment, she shut the door again, leaving him alone in the hallway. He retraced his steps back to the living room and scooped up his discarded pajamas. Well, what had he expected after he'd ruined the moment? A night of cuddling and maybe more lovemaking?

Unsure what their next encounter would bring, Keaton had a hard time falling asleep. Or maybe it was the way he kept reliving the taste of Lark and the feel of her curvaceous body beneath his. He remembered glancing at the clock around five-thirty. The next thing he knew it was seven-fifteen and he was running late.

Lark was in the kitchen, humming an off-key ditty when he emerged from his bedroom. She looked well rested and happy. Her cheeks wore a lovely shade of rose and her eyes danced in merriment as she alternately flipped French toast and tickled Grace.

The smell of bacon and fresh-brewed coffee hit his nose at the same time. His stomach growled in appreciation. The noise was loud enough to alert Lark that he was there. She poured him a cup of coffee and added the perfect amount of creamer. With a sweet-as-peaches smile she extended it to him.

"You look rested," he remarked over the rim of the mug.

"I conked out the second my head hit the pillow and slept until Grace woke me at quarter to six. That was almost five hours. I feel amazing."

Keaton considered his own restless night and grimaced. Obviously he'd been the one most impacted by their late night interlude. "I'm glad to hear that."

"I appreciate you getting up with her last night, but I'm off for the next few days, so you need to get a good night's sleep tonight."

So she was going to act as if nothing had happened? It was not how Keaton had imagined the morning going, but far less awkward than if they'd rehashed what had been a colossal mistake. And he wasn't just talking about their lack of protection. He should never have kissed her or let things get so out of hand that their first time together had been on the living room floor.

"I'm sure that's what will happen." Keaton's gaze wandered to the spot in the living room where they'd made love the night before. "Lark," he began, only to have her shake her head vigorously. "We should talk."

"Do you still want to come with me to Grace's checkup?" she asked. "It's at four."

"Yes." He watched her closely as she dished up

two slices of French toast and piled bacon on the side. The urge to kiss her rose in him so fast he was reaching for her before his conscious mind registered the impulse.

She blocked him with the plate. "Eat up. You have a busy day today. What time is the contractor expecting you at the ranch?"

"Nine."

"And then you've promised to help move the storage files at the town hall." She shooed him toward a bar stool and went to fill a travel mug with coffee. "How are things going with the cleanup?"

Obviously she was eager to get rid of him. Keaton wasn't sure whether or not that was a good sign. What had happened between them the night before bothered her more than she let on or she wouldn't be making such an obvious effort to act as if nothing had happened.

"Most of the big debris has been cleared. I'll know more when we get under the tarps they stretched over what used to be the records room and start moving the cabinets."

"I imagine some of those files go back to the 1800s."

Back to a time before the Holts and Taylors fought over two thousand acres of prime land. Land rich with the water so essential to sustain large herds of cattle through the dry season. Keaton's gut tightened at the reminder of how much animosity existed between their families. He hadn't been thinking about repercussions when he made love to Lark last night. Or the consequences of letting his feelings for her develop.

She wasn't her sister. Growing up, Skye had been confident and popular. The apple of her father's eye, she'd been unafraid of disappointing her parents. She'd loved Jake passionately and turned her back on everyone she cared about to be with him.

Lark wasn't like that. Brilliant, sensitive and mostly ignored by her parents, she'd been shy and reserved. If their families hadn't hated each other and his brother hadn't secretly been seeing her sister, he probably never would've noticed her. What a shame that would have been.

Much as Lark wasn't like Skye, Keaton wasn't like his brother. Jake could leave Royal and their ranch, knowing that Keaton would stick around to take charge. He doubted that Jake had ever considered whether Keaton wanted to do something else with his life. Or that their parents might desperately miss the younger Holt.

Damn. His brother could be a hardheaded, selfish idiot. When Jake finally showed up in Royal,

Keaton might have to take his brother down hard before letting him anywhere near Skye and Grace.

"Keaton?" Lark's worried voice broke through the haze of irritation that gripped him. "Are you okay?"

"Yeah. Fine." He rubbed his temple to ease the ache there. "I was just thinking about Jake."

"About beating him bloody?"

"What?" Her accurate read of his thoughts caught him off guard.

"You looked pretty angry." And from the look on her face, she'd been worried he was mad at her.

"Sorry. It's just every time I ask myself why he hasn't called or shown up, I can't imagine what could be keeping him away."

"Hopefully we'll find out sooner rather than later."

Once she'd gotten Keaton out the door, Lark released a gigantic sigh of relief. He'd so obviously wanted to rehash what had happened between them the night before and she wasn't sure she knew what to say.

Yes, it had been a mistake. A glorious, wonderful, spectacular mistake. One she'd repeat anytime and as often as she could.

Except she probably wouldn't get the chance.

She closed her eyes and let the memory of his hot kisses and fierce possession wash through her.

Nothing in her life came close to those moments he'd made love to her, and she wasn't sure how she was supposed to go forward.

With Grace's needs taken care of for the moment and a housekeeper coming in twice a week to cook, clean and do laundry, Lark found herself with a few precious hours of free time. Normally she would pick up a book and get lost among its pages, but her mind was far too restless to concentrate. Instead she carried Grace in her bouncy seat into her bedroom and went to investigate her closet.

One of the nice things about the years she hadn't lived in Royal was the freedom she'd enjoyed from her mother's criticism. Vera Taylor had an opinion about everything when it came to a person's appearance, and her daughters faced the lash of their mother's judgment the most. The constant badgering to *do something* about her appearance had turned Lark into an antifashionista.

All through high school, she'd owned several pairs of jeans and a variety of nondescript shirts that she rotated through her closet and the laundry. When it grew cold, she'd add a bulky hooded sweatshirt. In the summer she wore cutoffs and T-shirts. Her resolve to blend in drove her mother absolutely crazy. Vera lived to be complimented and envied for her carefully chosen outfits, flawless skin and perfect hair.

It wasn't until Lark arrived at college that things changed. Her freshman year roommate was a fashion major and had gently guided Lark to break out of her rut. Without being compared to her beautiful sister all the time, Lark had discovered a sense of confidence. Karen had shown her how wearing jeans with the right top and a cute pair of flats could make her feel pretty, even sexy. By the end of the first semester, she'd added several skirts and even a couple dresses to her wardrobe.

From the very back of her closet, Lark pulled out a garment bag. In it were four dresses that she hadn't worn since returning to Royal and one she'd never taken the tags off. She considered each one as she arranged them on her bed. Two were casual daytime dresses, something she'd wear to go shopping with friends or grab drinks at happy hour. The third one was a fancy cocktail dress she'd bought her senior year of college to attend a Christmas party at her boyfriend's law firm. Her gaze came at last to the fourth dress.

She'd bought it on Karen's recommendation because her roommate insisted that every woman needed an LBD in her closet. This particular little black dress showed off Lark's curves to great advantage. The wrap design drew attention to her hourglass shape and left her arms bare. Lark had never worn the dress because she felt so blatantly sexy in it, and that was significantly outside her comfort zone.

Lark stripped off her jeans and sweater and slipped the dress over her head. Before she looked at her reflection in the mirror, she fetched her one pair of heels. Basic black pumps that pushed her height over the six-foot mark. A pair of gold earrings completed the outfit. Gathering a deep breath, Lark regarded herself in her full-length mirror and gasped.

She looked amazing.

And not unlike herself, something she'd discovered the last time she'd tried on the dress. That had been four years ago, before she'd moved back to Royal. Returning to her hometown had caused Lark to regress into what had been comfortable and familiar. Once again she was that wallflower who worked hard and received little notice. She spent quiet nights at home reading or decorating cakes. Once in a while she went out with her coworkers, but she was never the girl men wanted to flirt with.

Now, for the first time in what seemed like forever, she craved someone's attention. Longed to see a man's eyes to light up when he spotted her.

For him to be a little tongue-tied when she smiled his way.

And she wanted that man to be Keaton Holt.

Keaton arrived home much later than he intended. He glanced at Lark's closed bedroom door before checking on Grace. The infant was sleeping peacefully in her crib. It was about half an hour before her four o'clock wellness visit.

Work at the town hall wasn't going well. The delicate process of unearthing over a century of the town's records had suffered yet another setback.

After a quick, hot shower Keaton put on a pair of khaki slacks, a striped shirt and a navy sweater. With the restaurants on the west side of town destroyed by the tornado, they had only the Royal Diner or Claire's to choose from. As much as he enjoyed the diner's fifties décor and terrific food, the place was a hotbed of local gossip. If he and Lark showed up there with Grace, they would be mobbed with questions and the focus of far too much speculation. Better that they dined at Claire's, which boasted a more refined ambience and an upscale menu.

Lark must have decided the same thing, because she was wearing a black trench coat and heels. His eyes were immediately drawn to her bare calves.

She had great legs. Long. Toned. He loved riding his hands up their smooth length, relishing the power of her muscles as she wrapped her thighs around his hips.

Desire pulsed through him, a languid, sensual tug on his hormones. Until they'd made love, he'd been mostly preoccupied by her perfect, luscious breasts. Now he was having trouble deciding which turned him on the most.

"Ready?" Lark questioned, picking up Grace's carrier and giving him a strange look. She'd dusted her eyelids with gray shadow and darkened her lashes with mascara, making her green eyes stand out. A soft pink gloss covered her lips, drawing his attention there next. "Grace's appointment is in ten minutes," she prompted, her voice edged with smoke.

There was something different about her today and it wasn't just the stylish trench or the makeup she'd applied. She wore confidence like a favorite accessory. He had a hard time keeping his thoughts from straying to what dinner might lead to.

"Here, let me take that." He relieved her of the carrier and gestured her ahead of him out the door.

Since Grace hadn't left the house since they brought her home from the hospital, her car seat was still in Keaton's truck. He settled her carrier into it and made sure everything was secure while Lark clambered into the passenger seat.

"Where to?" he asked, backing slowly down the driveway.

"The medical building just south of the hospital."

They rode in silence the ten minutes it took to navigate the short distance. Keaton kept his eyes on the road in front of them, but his attention was half on Lark. He was accustomed to her unadorned beauty, appreciated her naturalness, but the bombshell seated beside him was whipping up his appetite.

Once they were inside the lobby, they looked up the doctor's office on the wall directory and made their way there. "So, I was thinking Claire's for dinner," he said as they stepped off the elevator on the third floor. "We run a better chance of an uninterrupted meal."

"That sounds nice."

Her quiet reply nagged at him. She didn't seem withdrawn or angry with him, but the camaraderie they'd enjoyed these last ten days was missing. And he didn't like it one bit. He'd come to relish their particular blend of arguing and amity. Most days she kept him guessing and when she wasn't stimulating him intellectually, she was inspiring his baser urges.

"I thought since it's where Jake and Skye had their last official date in Royal," he said, holding the clinic's door open for her, "that it should be the place where we have our first."

She halted halfway to the receptionist's desk and gave him a blank stare. "Our first…?"

"Date."

"Can I help you?" the receptionist asked brightly.

"We have an appointment with Dr.—"

"Reedy," Lark supplied, her gaze not leaving Keaton's face.

"For our niece, Grace Holt-Taylor."

"If you can fill out this paperwork." The receptionist pushed a clipboard and a pen across the desk toward them. "I'll let the doctor know you're here."

Keaton sat beside Grace's carrier and watched Lark fill out the baby's pertinent details. As he waited for her to finish, he was bemused at the anxiety that tightened his chest. She'd been caught off guard when he described their dinner as a date, but she didn't protest the notion. Did that mean she was willing to give things between them a shot?

Before he found out, they were being escorted into a tiny exam room. The nurse who led them there brought in a scale and a tape measure to take Grace's measurements. Between them the nurse and Lark peeled Grace out of her fleece onesie. Not liking the cool air on her skin, Grace began to protest. In record time the stats were recorded on her chart and then the nurse left them alone to calm the baby.

Rather than dress her again, Lark wrapped Grace in a blanket and held her against her shoulder. It only took a bit of rocking for the infant to calm. Once the room was silent, Keaton spoke.

"I've spent the entire day thinking about you," he said. "I think we have a connection that goes beyond taking care of Grace or simple physical attraction." The words that had been racing through his mind all day spilled easily from his lips.

"I like you too," she said, her voice and expression solemn. "It's just that dating means we're going down a path that ended badly for Jake and Skye."

"They decided to run away from trouble rather than face it. We're both stronger than that."

"You might be, but then your parents are way more sensible and forgiving than mine."

The door opened before he could respond and Keaton was left to mull her words.

"Good afternoon, Lark," Dr. Reedy said, flashing his teeth in a boisterous grin. In his midfifties, the pediatric physician had pronounced crow's-feet at the corners of his eyes and strong laugh lines bracketing his mouth. He stuck his hand toward Keaton. "I'm Dr. Reedy."

"Keaton Holt."

The doctor nodded. "Grace's uncle. So, how is our little angel doing?"

Lark and Keaton spoke at once.

"Terrific."

"Wonderful."

"Fantastic," Dr. Reedy said. "Well, her weight has increased nicely. She's a little ahead of where we'd expect she'd be at this time."

Keaton appreciated that bit of good news. At least when his brother showed up, Keaton could feel confident that he'd done everything possible for Grace. "And her reflux?"

"We're still giving her the drops and that's working great."

"She's sleeping okay?"

Keaton and Lark exchanged glances.

"Pretty well," Keaton said. "At first she wanted to be held all the time, but she's adjusted to her bouncy chair and swing really well in the last few days."

"Sounds like everything is going nicely."

After that Dr. Reedy began his exam. Grace hated every second of being checked and let the entire building know. He had a list of questions for Lark and Keaton as he worked and they traded off answering.

"I'd say she's doing great," Dr. Reedy pronounced,

giving the two adults a pleased smile. "We'll need to see her in another month. You can schedule that before you leave."

From the way Lark's mouth drooped, Keaton suspected she was hoping her sister would be able to bring Grace to that checkup. Keaton agreed and hoped his brother was in town to drive her. The next time Keaton attended a baby wellness visit, he wanted it to be for his own son or daughter.

Eight

After leaving the doctor's office, Lark sat in the backseat of Keaton's truck and pulled out Grace's bottle.

"Do you want to skip the restaurant and do dinner at home?" Keaton offered, watching them from the front seat.

The baby was still agitated from being checked out by Dr. Reedy, but she quickly settled down. "I think she'll be okay after she has something to eat. She's really hungry these days. I've started preparing four-ounce bottles and she can almost get through the whole thing."

"It's amazing how much has changed in the ten days since she's left the hospital."

With the bottle half-consumed, Lark took it away and handed the baby and a burp cloth to Keaton.

"And who would've guessed you'd be so good with babies?"

"Certainly not me."

"I think your mother was a little shocked." As soon as Grace expelled the gas trapped in her stomach, Lark handed Keaton the bottle and let him finish the feeding.

Watching the two of them together, she noticed how her fondness for him increased a little more each day. If things kept going this way, she was going to start thinking in terms of the *L* word that wasn't *like*. To her surprise, this didn't give her the qualms it might have a week ago. For one thing, it wasn't as if she could stop the inevitable from happening. Keaton was a wonderful man with everything going for him. If she wasn't a Taylor falling for a Holt, she would feel free to revel in her happiness.

Lark executed a quick diaper change before Grace drifted off to sleep. "I think that will buy us a couple hours at least," she said, switching back into the passenger seat.

The late afternoon sun hit Keaton's blue eyes, making them glow. "Then we won't have to rush." He slipped on a pair of sunglasses and started the engine.

Finding herself oddly breathless, Lark clasped her hands together and set them in her lap. It was a good thing they were avoiding the Royal Diner's bright interior. At least in the soft lighting at Claire's her flushed skin and feverish gaze would be less obvious.

The hostess led them to a four-top toward the back and replaced one of the chairs with a stand that Grace's carrier fit into. While Keaton got Grace settled, Lark slipped out of her coat and draped it over the empty chair beside her. When Keaton looked in her direction, his eyes widened.

"You look amazing," he murmured, a hoarse note in his voice. "That dress suits you."

"I was worried it was too much." Lark ran her hands down the dress, smoothing the fabric over her hips. "I bought it in Houston but never had a reason to wear it."

"It's perfect."

She loved the way his gaze clung to her as she sat down and dropped the napkin in her lap. His intensity heightened her confidence and made it easy to shoot him a flirtatious glance.

"I haven't ever been here," she said, scanning the menu. "What do you suggest?"

"That we skip dinner and go straight home."

Her stomach executed a back flip. "But I'm hungry," she protested.

"So am I." And his steady regard left her no doubts about where his mind had gone.

Excited by the hot lust in his gaze, Lark surrendered to the smile tugging at her lips. Already she was on fire for him. Her nipples hardened against the silk of her bra. An ache throbbed between her thighs.

All her life she'd existed in her head. She read books and imagined faraway places she'd probably never visit. Baking cakes gave her a way to express her creative side, but it was a hobby that involved precise measuring and exact bake times. Her buttercream flowers were a work of art, but they took hours and meticulous attention to detail to get just right.

The way she felt around Keaton was so completely foreign. Her blood simmered. She grew rash and wild. They'd made love on her living room floor last night. Just ripped off their clothes and dove straight in. There'd been no preset number of dates before the event. Hell, they weren't even dating. She wanted him naked, his strong body heavy on her while he plunged into her over and over.

"Are you okay?"

Keaton's question broke through her sensual

fog. Unclenching her hands, she discovered half-moon indents in her palms where her fingernails had dug in. Lark picked up her water and sipped it. She wanted to put the cool glass against her heated cheeks, but that would be a dead giveaway. "I'm fine. Why?"

"You were staring into space with such a fierce expression on your face. What were you thinking about?"

Well, she certainly couldn't tell him the truth. "There's a woman I work with. She hates me." Lark was surprised by her own vehemence. She hadn't told anyone about her frustration with Marsha. It wasn't her style to complain.

"I can't imagine anyone hating you." Another man might have used that line to flirt. Keaton was completely serious. "You're kind, thoughtful and intelligent."

She wasn't upset that he didn't describe her as beautiful. She wasn't. Her mother was right to complain that she did nothing to make herself look more attractive. Besides, the way he focused all his attention on her was so much better than a bunch of flattery she wouldn't believe.

"I'm also efficient, hardworking and intolerant of people who don't pull their weight." Lark stared in fascination as Keaton's mouth curved into a wry line. "From the minute I walked into the ICU, she's acted like I'm the most annoying person she's ever met."

"So she's intimidated."

"Why should she be? She has seniority in the department and everyone except the head nurse defers to her."

"Everyone except the head nurse and you," Keaton guessed. His eyes glowed. He seemed to understand something Lark wasn't grasping.

"She's lazy and sloppy. I've tried to be nice, but I draw the line at pandering to her ego."

"And she's working in the ICU where your sister is. You told me you transferred from surgery to the ICU to watch over Skye. Why did you feel that was necessary?"

Lark caught her breath. Was that it? She didn't trust Marsha to take good care of Skye, and the other nurse had picked up on that? In the days following the tornado, Lark had been frantic about her sister's condition. She'd spent long hours at Skye's side, overseeing her care like a fierce mama bear. Looking back, Lark realized she probably hadn't made any of the nurses' lives easy, but Marsha's least of all because her level of care had been subpar in Lark's opinion.

A week later, Lark had requested a temporary

transfer to the ICU. Marsha couldn't have been happy. No wonder she'd been so unfriendly.

"I really need to work on my people skills," Lark muttered. "I did not connect the dots."

"How do you feel now?"

"Better. At least I have an idea why Marsha hates me. It will make dealing with her a lot easier."

Her father often complained about how aloof Keaton was. Said the Holt boy thought he was too good for any of them. After spending time with Keaton, Lark decided her father was wrong. Keaton didn't believe himself superior. Rather, he was focused on his ranch and spent more time thinking than talking. Thus, when he had something to say it was worth listening to.

During dinner their conversation turned to the town's recovery efforts and the projects Keaton had been involved in. Lark had no idea how much he'd pitched in.

"I haven't really kept up with what's been going on," Lark said, pushing vegetables around her plate. "I should've pitched in."

Keaton shook his head. "You've had your hands full taking care of Skye and watching over Grace and we haven't been short any volunteers."

"I feel like I should be doing something."

"Most of what's going on now involves demolition or construction, but I can check and see what other things might be available."

"That would be great."

Despite the easy flow of conversation during dinner, Lark's tension grew. They were minutes away from heading home and she hadn't yet figured out how to take advantage of the camaraderie they'd achieved. Her mind and body were eager for another round of lovemaking, but she didn't know how to go about communicating that to Keaton.

It didn't help that his relaxed manner gave no clue if his thoughts ran in the same direction. She declined dessert. Even if her mouth hadn't been dry and her stomach in knots, she wouldn't have enjoyed anything sweet. She was far too eager to get Keaton alone. Maybe in the privacy of her home she could tempt him to kiss her and maybe that would lead to more.

While they awaited the check, a dark-haired man clapped Keaton on the back, but the newcomer's curious gaze was fixed on Lark.

"Keaton, good to see you out enjoying yourself for a change."

"Hello, Gil." Keaton stood and greeted the tall man with a hearty handshake before turning in Lark's direction. "I'm not sure if you two have met. This is Lark Taylor." He gestured toward the carrier beside him. "And Grace, our niece. Lark, this is Gil Addison, president of the Texas Cattleman's Club."

"Both Keaton and my father have spoken of you." Lark smiled. "It's nice to put a face with a name."

"You're Tyrone's daughter?"

She nodded, seeing the way his eyes narrowed as if surprised she and Keaton were so relaxed with each other.

"Okay, date night is on." A tall woman with shoulder-length wavy brown hair appeared at Gil's side. "There's no emergency at home."

"This is my wife, Bailey," Gil said, putting his arm around her waist before finishing the introductions.

"Nice to meet you," Lark murmured, realizing how much she'd isolated herself these last few years.

The couples chatted for a few more minutes before Gil and Bailey returned to their own table where the waiter had just delivered their appetizer.

On the ride back to her house, Lark realized her earlier anxiety about the rest of the evening had dissipated. Gil Addison's surprise at finding her and Keaton together reminded Lark how many obstacles stood between them. Letting herself get further wrapped up with Keaton would be asking for trouble. She was better off chalking up their single encounter as a lightning strike. Life-altering and never to be repeated.

Keaton took charge of Grace as they entered the house and pushed Lark in the direction of her bedroom. "Go get into your pajamas," he commanded, no hint of playfulness anyway in his manner.

Her stomach clenched in reaction. "But it's not even seven o'clock."

"You owe me at least an hour of...what did you call it? Postcoital? You owe me an hour of postcoital snuggling."

"What are you talking about?" Heat rushed up her neck and set fire to her cheeks.

"You ran off before I had the chance to hold you in my arms and savor how great you smell and how soft your skin is."

Embarrassed laughter bubbled in her chest. "I ran off because you acted like an insensitive jerk."

"Stop trying to pick a fight with me or I'll change my mind about the pajamas and make you cuddle dressed exactly as you were when we ended."

Unsure why he thought threatening her with snuggling naked was at all intimating, Lark decided not to argue further. What was the point when all she wanted was for him to hold her in his manly arms and kiss her breathless?

Since the pajama top she'd been wearing the night

before was ruined, Lark had to find something else to put on. Most of what she wore in the winter she'd purchased to combat the cool nights, and she didn't like the notion of her skin being so completely inaccessible.

"That's not what you were wearing last night," he said as he showed up in her bedroom, wearing pretty much the same pajama bottoms he'd had on the night before.

"You tore off the buttons, remember?" She glanced down at the sleeveless cotton nightgown. "It might not be pajamas, but it's sleepwear."

His frown told her he wasn't fully convinced, but he held out his hand. "Do you want to do this here or on the couch?"

Although the couch's limited space would force their snuggling to be extra close, she preferred the bed's potential. "Here."

"A good choice." Lifting her off her feet as if she weighed no more than a dry leaf, Keaton placed her in the middle of the mattress and settled down beside her. He put his arm around her and pulled her against his side.

She laid her cheek against his shoulder but had a hard time relaxing. Hunger raged through her, firing her blood and awakening an insistent thrumming in her loins. While cuddling with him had sounded wonderful, what she really wanted was his hands on her skin, driving her mad with pleasure.

"What's wrong?" he asked, his voice deep and content.

Lark shook her head slightly and gazed up at him. His eyes were closed. She envied his tranquility.

"It just doesn't seem like this is how we would have ended up last night."

"Why not?"

"Something about it doesn't feel organic."

"Organic?" The corners of his mouth twitched. "What do you suggest?"

"I think we should get into the position we were in just after we finished last night and take it from there."

He cracked one eye open and regarded her for a long moment. Then with a huge sigh, he sat up. "I just have one question." He paused and let his fingers drift down her cheek. "With clothes or without."

"Definitely without."

And just like that they were kissing and rolling across her mattress, shedding her nightgown and his pajamas. The foreplay was feverish and focused, leaving little breath for words. And just when Lark thought she was going to explode with anticipation, Keaton sheathed himself in one of the condoms she'd squirreled away in her nightstand and slid inside her. Their breath mingled as they rode the escalating waves of pleasure. If it had been great last night, it was even better now because they were just a little bit more familiar with each other.

Lark climaxed first, her body reaching completion mere seconds before Keaton pounded to his own finish. With their energy deliciously depleted, Keaton rolled onto his back and draped Lark's boneless body across his chest.

"You were right," he agreed, lifting her hair aside so he could deposit a kiss on her damp cheek. "This is much more organic."

"I knew it would be," she murmured, convinced that she could stay like this forever. "I was feeling really awkward before because I didn't know where to put my legs or the best place for my hands. Now I can't feel either, so it really doesn't matter."

Beneath her cheek his chest lifted and fell with his chuckle. "I have a great antidote for that when you're ready."

"I'm sure you do." She nuzzled his throat and smiled.

Already fresh desire was stirring at the edge of her consciousness. Her hunger for Keaton astonished her. In the past she'd never been driven by a need to tear someone's clothes off and have sex at the spur of the moment. She'd enjoyed intimacy with the men she dated, but the lovemaking was more like canoeing on a calm lake compared to the ocean storm she enjoyed with Keaton.

"Next weekend Paige Richardson is throw a party at the Double R to celebrate her barn raising," Keaton said, his fingers trailing a soothing path up and down Lark's back.

"Hmmm." Mesmerized by Keaton's caress, she had little more to offer.

For the last three months there'd been a lot of opportunities for the townsfolk to pitch in and help each other out. She knew the co-owners of R&N Builders, Aaron Nichols and his business partner, Colby Richardson, brother of Paige's deceased husband, had assisted Keaton with some aspects of rebuilding the Holt ranch house and outlying buildings. But with the high amount of devastation suffered throughout the town, the professional builders were spread thin.

So anyone with a free day or afternoon and a willingness to wield a hammer or a saw could easily find a project to work on. Lark knew Keaton had hosted a party at his place the weekend the town gathered to help with the roofing of the ranch house and his main barn.

"I think we should go together," Keaton continued. "And bring Grace."

Lark's contentment vanished as anxiety flared. "Sure."

"You don't sound convinced it's a good idea."

"I thought we were going to keep our situation as quiet as possible."

"We're co-caretaking Grace," he reminded her. "We were seen having dinner together at Claire's. I'm living with you. You don't think that speculation about us has circled town three times already?"

"You're right." But as long as she didn't have to confront a bunch of knowing smiles, she could at least pretend that no one would run to her parents with the news that she'd invited the family enemy to live with her.

Keaton kissed her shoulder. "You know I'm here for you, right?"

Lark knew his promise wasn't given lightly. Even though his parents hadn't treated her with the same disdain shown by Tyrone and Vera, Lark had gotten the distinct impression that they were hoping nothing was going on between her and Keaton. They didn't want to lose another son to a Taylor girl. With the feud between the families, it would be just a matter of time before conflict arose again, and that would mean trouble for everyone involved.

"What's bothering you?" Keaton asked.

"Nothing."

"You've sighed four times in the last two minutes."

"I'm really relaxed."

"They weren't sighs of contentment. You're worrying about something."

"I was just thinking your parents wouldn't be overly pleased to learn we've taken playing house—literally."

"You're wrong. They like you."

"Sure, as the woman who's taking care of their granddaughter. Not as the woman in their son's bed."

"Technically their son is in your bed."

She made a sour face at him. "It's not like you to take things so lightly." And then it occurred to her that she had no idea if that was true. How much did she really know about the man sprawled naked beneath her?

"Uh-oh. What now?"

"I'm just realizing how little I know about you."

"You know more than most."

"I do?" She considered what she'd learned in the last ten days.

"Why do I keep to myself?"

"Your ranch keeps you busy. You like your own

company. I've heard you make polite conversation if you have to, but I think you prefer more straightforward discussions."

"I dislike pretending to feel something I don't, and often that rubs people the wrong way."

People like her father, Lark realized. Tyrone Taylor never appreciated when the reality of a situation conflicted with his version of the truth.

"We've got that in common," Lark admitted, thinking back to those awful days after Skye ran off with Jake. "Sometimes I miss social cues, and that gets me into trouble. Luckily most people take me at face value, but once in a while, I encounter someone who takes offense at my cluelessness." Like Marsha at work, who needed the entire world to revolve around her. "Sometimes it's just easier being alone."

"You've felt like that for a long time. I remember as a kid you were always in your own world, either reading or standing around with a grumpy look on your face. What were you thinking about?"

"Usually stuff I'd been reading about earlier or how long before I could escape whatever I'd been dragged to."

He laughed. "Did that happen a lot?"

"Less as I got older. Most of the time when I was

a kid, my parents forgot I existed. The older I grew, the more invisible I became."

"That can't possibly be true."

"It is. Skye could have been an only child for all the impact I made on their lives." Lark shook her head, remembering how she'd alternated between resenting her younger sister and rejoicing that Skye was their mother's focus. "The times I remember being most happy were when I was lost in a story. While Mom coached Skye on her pageant walk or spent hours trying out new hairstyles or planning the next routine, I was up in my room or down by the creek, reading."

"I remember Jake complaining about you all through school."

"Complaining about me?" She thought back to those days and couldn't remember ever so much as making eye contact with him even though they'd been in the same grade and he'd been so friendly with her sister. "Why?"

"The teachers were always using your work as an example. You weren't just bright, you worked really hard."

"I don't know that I worked all that hard. I just made sure I got everything done. It's an easy thing to do when you're inept socially and have only a handful of equally awkward friends to hang out with."

"What else do you know about me?"

"You do crossword puzzles in pen. Most people would find that impressive."

"But not you?"

"I've known for a long time that you're extremely smart. In fact, there were a lot of people who figured you'd end up in a think tank somewhere after you graduated from UC Berkeley."

"I had offers, but in the end what I really wanted was to come back to Royal and ranch."

"I understand that. For a year I considered staying in Houston, but my heart was here." And no one was more surprised by that fact than Lark. All through high school she'd been eager to get away. Only it was a case of the grass not necessarily being greener on the other side. "But do you ever feel as if you wasted four years getting a degree in mathematics?"

"It's actually worse than that," he said, looking slightly abashed. "I completed my master's and began working on my doctorate."

"Wow." She regarded him in amazement. "But you prefer ranching?"

"I'm not built to spend my days indoors. Ranching suits me. And before you think I've completely wasted my education, I do consulting work for a company outside Boston."

"When do you find time?"

"Evenings. Anytime I need a break from the ranch. Meeting deadlines has been challenging in the days since the storm, but the only thing that's suffered has been my social life." His expression grew momentarily wry. "Which isn't saying much."

"We are a lot more alike than I realized." Lark regarded him with a sinking heart. The compatibility between them was going to lead to deeper feelings. How could she help but fall for him? He was handsome. Brilliant. And he understood her.

"I wonder what would have happened if we'd been closer in age the way Jake and Skye were," he mused, echoing something she'd caught herself pondering several times in the last few weeks.

"You mean would we have become friends against our parents' wishes?" She shook her head. "I was too sure your family was evil." And too afraid of disappointing her father.

"And now?"

"The feud might have started for a good reason, but it's idiotic that we haven't found a way to settle things. Your parents have done a better job supporting Skye and Grace than my own, and that makes them friend, not foe, in my book."

"And me?"

Her gaze met his. The concern darkening his eyes to a somber shade of blue made her heart lose its rhythm.

"You know how I feel about you."

"I really don't." This wasn't a flirtatious game. He was regarding her as if he really wanted to hear her opinion.

How much did she dare tell him?

"I like you."

"Just like?"

Although there was a trace of amusement in his tone, Lark couldn't tear her gaze from his. "Very much like. I wouldn't have…you know…"

"Made love?"

"Exactly. It's not something I do lightly." Or often. "When I'm with you I believe I can handle everything."

"We've made a good team."

But it was a temporary alliance. Soon Skye would wake and take Baby Grace back to wherever she'd been living. Or Jake would come to town in search of his daughter and the woman he loved and reawaken old hurts. Her parents would demand that Lark stand at their side once more. Against her sister and the Holts.

"What are you worrying about?" Keaton asked.

"I'm not Skye," she explained. "I've never had the strength to go against my parents." She snuggled her cheek against his shoulder, ashamed at her weakness. "If they find out about us, I'm not sure my choices will make you happy."

Beneath her, Keaton's chest rose as he gathered a great breath in his lungs. "You don't know what's going to happen or when. Until then let's make sure we make the most of the present."

Nine

Lark's home sparkled with cleanliness and order by Wednesday night. Despite the already pristine nature of the housekeeping, Lark had attended to every corner and out of the way surface to make sure it was free of dust and dirt.

It hadn't been Keaton's intention that she work like a maniac in advance of his parents' visit, but every attempt to make her stop was met with stony determination.

"Enough," he commanded, plucking the surface cleaner and rag from her hands and dragging her from the kitchen. Scooping Grace from her swing, he handed her to Lark. It was the only way to pause her obsessive housework. "My mother is not going to notice your house. She'll have eyes only for Grace."

"Does she look okay?"

The dress Lark had bought for Grace was pale pink with a scalloped hem and white flowers embroidered on the bodice. Her hair had grown noticeably in the last couple weeks, but the fine texture and white-blond color didn't make it seem as if she had much going on. Lark fussed with the tiny rosebud clip she'd attached to the silky strands.

"She's perfect," Keaton assured her, refraining from adding that his mother wouldn't judge what her granddaughter was wearing.

The doorbell rang, announcing his parents' arrival.

Lark started at the sound and gazed frantically toward her front door. "Maybe you should hold her?"

"Relax." He tilted Lark's chin up and kissed her softly, letting his lips linger far longer than he'd intended. "Everything is going to be fine."

He left Lark standing in the middle of the living room, a dazed expression on her flushed face, and went to welcome his parents. He wasn't surprised when his mother brushed right past him with barely a hello and went in search of Grace. The intensity on her face as she approached the pair made Lark's body stiffen.

"There she is." Gloria stopped short of plucking Grace from Lark's arms, but touched the infant's cheek with gentle fingertips. "Oh, she's absolutely precious. And I think she looks a little like Jake through the chin."

"Would you like to hold her?"

"You're sure it's okay?" Keaton's mother looked delighted.

Lark's gaze went past Gloria and fastened on her son. "Absolutely."

Grace barely stirred as she went from her aunt to her grandmother. Hearing the volley of questions begin, Keaton turned to his father and gestured with his head toward the kitchen.

"I think they'll be occupied for some time. Can I get you a beer?"

His dad grinned. "Always."

Keaton showed his father the steaks he'd bought for later and David Holt nodded approvingly over the thick cuts. Although Keaton had insisted that Lark didn't need to worry about fixing dinner, she'd made half a dozen side dishes to accompany the main course from two types of potatoes to three cold salads.

"How are things going?" Keaton's father nodded toward Lark.

"Fine." His gaze lingered on the pair of women in

fond amusement. "Taking care of a newborn, and a preemie at that, has been easier than I expected."

"And the Taylor girl?"

Something in his father's tone set Keaton's radar buzzing. "You mean Lark? What about her?"

"You're living here, right?"

"Yes."

What was his father getting at?

"She's a lot prettier than I remember."

"Your point?" Keaton quizzed, although he had a pretty good idea what was on his father's mind.

"Just want to make sure you know what you're doing."

Having his father doubt his judgment took Keaton by surprise. "Why would you think I don't?"

"Don't take that tone with me," his father said. "Your brother got involved with a Taylor girl and look what happened."

So his father had learned nothing in the last four years. "Seems to me he's been living quite happily with the woman he loves," Keaton retorted, making no effort to moderate his irritation.

"You don't know that. We haven't had any contact with him in four years. Anything could have happened."

"They have a beautiful baby girl. That speaks for Jake and Skye still being together."

"Then why isn't he here?" Grief showed in David Holt's gaze. "If they're so happy, why hasn't he made any attempt to be here for Skye and Grace?"

"The investigator I hired was able to find out Jake is in the Middle East, he just doesn't know where yet."

"I don't understand why his assistant won't just give you his number."

"She…." Keaton hesitated, unsure if his mother had shared the next part with his father. "Told me when I identified myself that Jake didn't have a brother."

David sucked in a sharp breath. "Did you tell that to your mother?"

"She knows."

"One of you should have told me." The news had obviously landed a huge blow to Keaton's father.

"I honestly thought he'd be here by now and that there wouldn't be anything to tell."

"I'll call her," Keaton's father said. "She'll give me his number or I'll—"

"David," Gloria called. "Come over here and hold your granddaughter."

"Mom already tried calling," Keaton told his father. "The assistant won't budge. There's something a little off with her."

His father snorted. "A little?"

"The investigator will find him," Keaton said, sounding more confident than he felt.

"See that he does." With those parting words David crossed to where his wife snuggled their granddaughter. Lark offered a shy smile as she passed Keaton's father. He responded with a brief nod. While she bustled about the kitchen, pulling out side dishes and heating the oven, Keaton assessed her state of mind. She was looking agitated again. He had to block her between his body and the counter in order to gain her attention.

"Relax," he said.

"You keep saying that, but it's not going to happen." She scowled at him. "Do you think I didn't notice the way your father was looking at me? He isn't happy about our arrangement."

"He said you were pretty."

The stern look Lark leveled at him would have started a lesser man sputtering apologies. "And then proceeded to warn you that Taylor girls bring Holt boys nothing but heartache?"

"Not in so many words."

Lark set her hand on his stomach, intending to push him away. Keaton grabbed her wrists and pulled her arms around his waist. She stiffened, but he held firm.

"They'll see," she hissed.

He couldn't care less. When Jake and Skye had fallen in love, the connection between their feuding families began to transform. With Grace's arrival, there was yet another string binding them together. A sound relationship between Keaton and Lark would put an end to multiple generations of fighting.

"That's the idea." And then he kissed her.

Her lips quickly grew pliant and responsive. He kept the contact romantic, ignoring the passion that flared between them. There would be time enough to satisfy that later. When he was sure he'd made his point, he released her and stepped back.

"Keaton?" His mother's voice had a slight warble as she spoke his name.

"Yes, Mom?" He kept his gaze on Lark, letting her glimpse what was in his heart.

"Are you and Lark...together?"

He shifted one eyebrow up and waited for Lark to tell him what to answer. Her nod was barely perceptible, but it released all the tension in his muscles. "Yes. We are."

Lark's whole body felt as if it was on fire, although whether desire or embarrassment was the dominant cause, she wasn't sure.

"Okay, you've made your point," Lark muttered

to Keaton, stepping around him to go back to dinner preparations. She didn't glance into the great room to see how Gloria and David Holt reacted to their son's announcement. She imagined their faces reflected horror.

"Is this a new development?" Gloria sounded closer than she'd been moments earlier.

Unsure what she should contribute to the conversation, Lark kept her back to her guests and focused on getting her side dishes into the oven. She still had a green salad to pull together. After agonizing over which recipe would be best received, she decided to go with a simple collection of lettuce, carrots, grape tomatoes and cucumber. Along with that, she'd offer four different types of salad dressing.

When she'd told Julie about her limited entertaining experience and tools, the research assistant reached out to the surgical nurses for help. They'd plied her with serving dishes and favorite recipes. Lark had come home with more than enough to satisfy Keaton's parents.

"Relatively," Keaton said. "We were three years apart in school and never had a chance to get to know each other. If not for Grace's arrival, our paths might never have crossed."

With everything as ready as it could be for the moment, Lark had no more excuses to avoid her guests. "Can I get you something to drink?" she asked Gloria. "Water? Soda? Tea? Coffee? Wine?" She ran out of offerings and snapped her mouth shut.

"I have a bottle of your favorite Shiraz," Keaton suggested.

"Maybe with dinner. For now I'll take a glass of water."

"Flat or sparkling?"

"Sparkling."

"Plain? Lemon? Raspberry?"

Gloria shot her son an amused look. "No wonder you like her. She's prepared for everything."

Lark's cheeks burned, but the remark hadn't been unkind. "I wanted to make sure I had a variety of things on hand."

"Lemon." Gloria stepped into the kitchen and shooed her tall son out. "What can I do to help?"

Lark hovered near the refrigerator, a glass in one hand, a bottle of water in the other. "With ice or without?"

"Without is fine." Keaton's mother relieved her of the items with a gracious smile. "What can I do to help?" she repeated.

Knowing she would be all thumbs with Gloria in the kitchen, Lark gave her head a vigorous shake. "You came here to see your granddaughter, not to help me. Dinner's in great shape. Most everything is ready to go."

"Good. Then you can come sit with me and tell us everything about you."

Although Lark wanted to protest, Keaton's mother had her neatly trapped.

"There's not much to tell." She glanced at Keaton's father, noting his stern expression, and wished she was anywhere but here.

"I'm sure that's not the case," Gloria replied, drawing Lark onto the couch and motioning for her husband to hand over Grace. "David, why don't you go help Keaton with the steaks? You know how I like mine cooked."

Lark was able to relax a little when the Holt men headed out back to the enormous grill Keaton had recently purchased. David Holt so obviously disapproved of her and Keaton being together. She wasn't yet sure where Gloria's opinion lay, but she suspected she was about to find out.

"My son is obviously taken with you."

"I care for Keaton a great deal. I'm not going to hurt him. I hope you know that." The three rapid-fire sentences left Lark breathless. She stared at Grace, longing for an ounce of the baby's current tranquility.

"We've upset you. I'm sorry about that. It's just

that learning about your relationship with our son like this has come as a little bit of a shock."

As much as Lark wanted to let her guard down with Gloria, she'd been fooled by someone's appearance of niceness before. Not that she thought Keaton's mother was manipulative. With her thoughts spinning in confused circles, Lark kept her lips pressed together.

The silence didn't seem to bother Gloria. "I don't want you to think that we're prejudiced against your relationship with Keaton because you're a Taylor." She paused. "Well, perhaps my husband is a little distressed... But some of what's caught us off guard is that Keaton has always been a private person. We know he dates, but he hasn't brought a single girl around since high school. He must be pretty serious about you to share with us what's going on between you." She paused again to let her words sink in. "And so soon. How long have you been...seeing each other?"

Lark had a strong desire to shift uncomfortably, and held still with effort. "A couple weeks. Since he moved in here. I know things seem like they're happening fast, but I'm not sure Keaton is as serious as you think. We've been thrown together by circumstances."

But in truth, she wasn't sure how Keaton felt. He

made love to her with tenderness and passion, but that was in his nature. Lark doubted Keaton had left a string of casual one-night stands in his wake. At the same time, he was a man and not exactly ruled by his emotions. For one thing, she was pretty certain that of the two of them, she was the one falling harder.

"Is that how you feel about him?" Gloria asked. "That this is just a convenient fling?"

This wasn't a conversation Lark wanted to be having with Keaton's mother. Surely Gloria would understand that what happened between Lark and Keaton should remain between them.

"Neither one of us has spoken about the future. Right now we're focused on Grace." That said, Lark stood. "I'd better get everything ready. Those steaks are going to be done in no time, and I would hate for them to get cold while we wait for the rest of the food."

Lark didn't care that her retreat was graceless and desperate. She was prepared to satisfy the Holts' culinary preferences and assure them her housekeeping skills were adequate. What she hadn't equipped herself to do was explain what was happening between her and Keaton.

"You look a little pale," he remarked as he came in to get the steaks.

"Your mother had questions about what's going on with us."

"What did you tell her?"

His frank curiosity irritated her. "That I had to get dinner ready. Can we talk about this later?"

"Did you mention that I have a hard time keeping my hands off you?" He took her backside in one large hand and gave a provocative squeeze.

The urge to laugh struck her. "Stop it this instant." She kept her voice neutral and low so his mother wouldn't know anything untoward was going on. "What has gotten into you?" Where was the solitary man who spoke little and kept everyone guessing?

The wicked glint in his eyes faded. "I'm sorry my mom gave you a hard time. I've already explained to my father that I won't tolerate any attempts to make you uncomfortable. I'll drop off the steaks with him and have the same chat with my mom."

His earnest declaration made her head spin. No one had ever jumped to her defense before.

"Oh, please don't." The last thing Lark wanted was for Keaton's relationship with his parents to suffer because she couldn't handle a little admonishment. "She's just worried about you. Besides, don't forget I've been dealing with my mother, the tiger lady, all my life. By comparison your mom's a pussy cat."

He scrutinized her face for a long moment. "Are you sure?"

"Positive."

But it was nice that he wanted to defend her. It was something she could get used to. Not that she should. She was telling the truth when she'd told his mother that they hadn't discussed the future.

Proximity lust. She could never have used the term with Gloria, but it was an obvious explanation for what was going on with Keaton. Two people of the opposite sex thrown into everyday contact with each other. It was only a matter of time before desire exploded between them.

But while proximity lust described how the sparks had ignited between them, Lark wasn't sure it justified why her desire for Keaton grew stronger each day or how badly it made her heart hurt when she imagined living alone in her house once more. That was more likely caused by how hard she was falling for him.

Keaton steered his truck into an empty space along the Richardsons' driveway and cut the engine. Since the dinner with his parents, Lark had grown even more difficult to read, but not impossible. Looking at her now, he could tell she was a nervous wreck. A classic introvert, she'd admitted she wasn't at her best in crowds. And their very public appearance together was going to cause rampant speculation.

He lifted Lark's hand and dusted a kiss across her knuckles. Her arm muscles jerked at the contact. She scanned the area around the truck as if searching for someone. A second later she slipped her hand free.

"Sorry," she said, her voice husky with embarrassment. "I guess I'm a little more wound up than I thought."

"You know it's going to be okay, right?"

"Not if my parents are here."

"Chances are they won't be since neither of them has been any help in the recovery efforts and this party is to thank everyone who helped raise the Richardsons' barn." Keaton kept reproach from his tone as he pointed out her parents' shortcomings, but Lark looked as if she'd been kicked in the gut. "I'm not saying anything you don't already know."

"You're right." She shot him a half smile. "I think this is the first time I'm glad my parents are so self-absorbed."

Keaton detached Grace's carrier from the car seat and met Lark by the hood. As much as he wanted to hold her hand the way he had during the drive from her house, he sensed she needed him to maintain a casual distance. Not easy, considering the way her perfume made his head spin and her soft skin begged to be caressed.

As they strolled through the guests, Keaton noticed almost the entire Texas Cattleman's Club membership was in attendance. Often since the tornado had struck Royal, Keaton was glad he'd joined the club. His original purpose for joining hadn't been social. Making small talk to pass the time wasn't his idea of fun. Sure, he'd sometimes found the other members a good source of information on the market.

But in the beginning, he'd joined because he knew it would drive Tyrone Taylor crazy.

"People are staring at us," Lark murmured, her eyes darting from one group to another.

Keaton saw curiosity and speculation in the expressions of the folks they passed. "Maybe if we stopped and spoke with someone, we could answer the questions on everyone's mind."

"Like who?"

He scanned the crowd and spotted a likely pair of candidates. "How about Drew and Beth?" Keaton switched direction without waiting for Lark's response. Her discomfort worried him. He didn't want her to feel like a fish in an aquarium.

"Keaton, we haven't seen much of you lately,"

Drew said, reaching his hand out. "How are things going at the ranch?"

"Coming along. The outbuildings will be finished the end of next week, and the interior work is beginning on the house."

"That's great."

"Drew and Beth, you remember Lark Taylor. And this is our niece, Grace."

"I heard what happened to your sister," Beth said, peering into the carrier Keaton held. "Oh, she's darling. But so tiny."

"She was ten weeks premature," Lark explained, her voice soft and hesitant. "But she's doing really well."

Beth paused in her cooing at the baby. "How's Skye?"

Lark sighed. "She's still in a coma. Dr. Wakefield, the trauma surgeon who saved her life, said with the type of brain injury Skye has, she could wake anytime."

Or not at all.

Keaton knew what Lark feared. She'd broken down and spoken of her anxiety two nights ago after spending an hour sitting at her sister's bedside. All the pressure of Skye's coma and Grace's early birth, not to mention her parents' inflexible attitude toward their daughter and grandchild, was taking its toll.

"I hope it's soon. This beautiful baby needs her mama." Beth caught the attention of a redhead with long straight hair and bright green eyes. Megan McGuire, manager of Royal Safe Haven, the local animal shelter. "Megan, come meet Lark and her niece, Grace."

"Why don't I take Grace for a while?" Lark suggested to Keaton, her eyes brighter than they'd been a few minutes ago. She looked more confident since running into Beth. "Would you mind putting my cake on the dessert table?"

"Not at all." Although he'd promised not to leave her side, she was obviously comfortable enough to send him away. They exchanged burdens and Keaton headed toward the heavily laden food tables with Drew strolling beside him.

"Forgive my curiosity," Drew said, "but did you introduce Grace as your niece, as well?"

"Lark's sister and my brother, Jake, left town together four years ago. Grace is their daughter."

"Interesting. And now you and Lark?"

This was where things got sticky. Lark wanted to keep the truth hidden. Keaton wanted to shout his happiness from the rooftops. An unusual urge for him.

"We're just co-caretaking Grace until Skye wakes up or my brother gets to town."

"Oh." Drew frowned. "Sorry. I assumed you two were together."

Was the horse breeder unusually perceptive or were Keaton and Lark giving off a couple vibe? Knowing that wouldn't make her happy, he frowned.

"Are we that obvious?" Keaton asked with a low laugh. "I was trying hard to behave."

"Maybe not obvious to everyone." Drew glanced around. "But ever since Beth and I got together, I see budding romances everywhere I turn."

"Really?"

Keaton looked around. "I guess a few couples have fallen in love since the tornado." Besides Drew and Beth, their acting mayor, Stella Daniels, and Aaron Nichols were such a couple. "It makes sense. Tragedy can bring out strong emotions."

"And with so many people thrown together who wouldn't normally be." Drew paused. "Like you and Lark. Don't the Holts and Taylors have some dispute between you?"

"A long-standing feud over land. It's kept our families fighting for years."

"That must have been hard on your brother and Lark's sister."

"They left town because of it."

Keaton understood Lark's worry. Unlike his sibling, Keaton let his responsibilities keep him tied to the Holt Ranch and by extension the town. Nor did he think Lark had any desire to live elsewhere. They were committed here. Sacrifices would be necessary if they intended to be together. At this point he was pretty sure whom she'd choose between her family and him.

"That's tough," Drew said.

"I could use a beer." Keaton checked to see how Lark was doing and found her surrounded by women. "How about you?"

"Sounds great."

It took Keaton another forty-five minutes to make his way back to Lark's side. By the time he reached her, he expected she'd be furious that he'd left her, but she simply took his arm and smiled up at him.

"You two doing okay?" he asked, peering at a sleeping Grace.

"Just fine."

"Sorry I was gone so long."

"It's okay. You'd have been bored standing around while all the women oohed and aahed over Grace and asked dozens of questions about preemies."

"I'm sure you had answers for each and every one of their questions."

"Of course." A smile flitted across her lips, catching his attention. "We're experts now, aren't we?"

"We're getting there." He'd known that inviting her to accompany him today had been a risk, but so far it seemed to be paying off.

"And Grace wasn't the only thing they wanted to know about," she said, a hint of slyness in her tone. "A few asked if you and I were together."

"What did you tell them?"

"What we agreed on." Basically the same thing he'd told Drew.

"And that satisfied them?"

"Of course not. Each and every one believes you and I are together."

Her matter-of-factness confused him. Wasn't this what she'd been most afraid of?

"Are you worried it will get back to your parents?"

"I knew it would when I agreed to come."

"So why did you?"

"I've been really happy these last couple weeks, and that's because of you."

He didn't push her for more. "You and I are good for each other."

"And we're not the only ones who think so."

He doubted that would be enough to sustain her when her parents began pummeling her with their negative opinions. "Drew asked me if we were together too. He said since he and Beth have fallen in love he's paying more attention to the relationships around him."

"It's funny that he would say that," Lark said. "I've noticed myself being more interested in other people's love lives. There's a few people here who've started dating recently. And I can't help wondering if something is going on between Paige Richardson and her brother-in-law."

Keaton glanced over at their hosts. "Like what?"

"Not like they're together," Lark assured him, but frowned thoughtfully. "They're really in sync. I suppose it could be shared grief over losing someone they both love. Except I think Paige is less sad than she used to be. Is that weird?"

Now that Lark had pointed it out, Keaton noticed the way Colby stayed close beside his brother's widow but never touched her. Not even a casual brush of arms or hands. It was as if he took care to maintain space between them.

"Not weird. But maybe we've fallen prey to the same affliction that Drew has?"

"But Drew and Beth are in love," Lark began, her voice trailing off as she caught Keaton's gaze.

"Why don't we say our goodbyes and get out of here?" Keaton suggested, letting her glimpse the flash of sexual intent in his eyes. Suddenly he was very impatient to get her home. "I think Grace has had enough excitement for one day, don't you?"

"Sure." But she sounded a little nervous as she agreed. She sucked her lower lip between her teeth as her color began to rise.

"I think everyone will understand that preemies are more delicate than the average newborn."

"They are." Her gaze clung to his. "It was good to bring her out, but I don't want to push it."

"Absolutely." To anyone listening nearby, their conversation would seem mundane enough, but heat flared between them at their unspoken accord. "I'm glad we're in agreement."

Ten

Lark entered Royal Safe Haven in a distracted state. Even after a fifteen-minute drive, her body still hummed from Keaton's goodbye kiss. At Paige Richardson's party, Lark had met Megan McGuire, the shelter's manager, and agreed to volunteer with the dogs for a couple hours. Basically, they needed some human contact, a little fussing over.

Keaton had encouraged her to go. For the last three and a half months, Lark's entire world had been the hospital, her comatose sister and Baby Grace. He'd insisted that doing something outside her narrow world would clear her head. Lark felt guilty for leaving him alone with Grace again on the heels of four days of twelve-hour shifts at the hospital, but secretly she'd been excited to try something new.

Almost immediately she was struck by a sense of sadness that so many pets had lost their owners because of the tornado or other hardships. In the days following the storm, her focus had been Skye and Grace. She'd spent all her time at the hospital, either working or alternating between the two intensive care units. Except for the damage done to the hospital's west wing and the branches down all around in her neighborhood, Lark hadn't seen the town's widespread devastation.

Stories had filtered through the hospital of the fine job Stella Daniels had done working with FEMA, the National Guard and local agencies to bring in the help they needed. The Texas Cattleman's Club had stepped up and organized many of the cleanup projects around town. Colby Richardson and his partner had brought their construction expertise from Dallas to assist in the repair and rebuild efforts.

All this made Lark wish she'd pitched in more.

"Hi, Lark. Thanks for coming." Megan came out from the back, her smile welcoming and addictive. "Let me show you around."

The tour was brief and informative. By the end,

Lark was really glad she'd come. "What do you want me to do?"

"We've got a couple dogs that aren't adapting very well to being locked up. They'd love a twenty-minute walk."

"That sounds easy enough."

The first dog she walked was a beagle mix named Bugsy that started out by dragging her down the street. Before she'd left, Megan had handed her a pouch with dog treats and offered a brief lesson on loose leash training. By the end of the twenty minutes, Lark was surprised that the dog had stopped sniffing every tree and bush and was paying attention to her.

"Nice job." Megan approached while Lark was returning the dog to its pen. "Feel like trying another?"

"Sure."

The next dog Megan picked for her was an Australian shepherd. The shelter manager described the dog's color as red merle. She had a mottled blond and chestnut coat with touches of white.

"Aussies are incredibly smart and used for herding," Megan explained. "Nicki was Agnes Baker's dog. Agnes's place was hit by the tornado and she was badly hurt. I know it just about killed her to leave Nicki behind when she went to live with her daughter in Dallas, but there was no way she could take her along. For a couple months I'd hoped that Agnes would make a full recovery and come back to Royal, but her healing is progressing slower than anyone hoped."

Suddenly Lark was fighting back tears. "Oh, that's terrible."

Megan nodded. "Nicki is a great dog. Where we run into problems with her is that she's too smart for most people. And she's used to a lot of exercise, so she gets destructive if left on her own for eight or more hours a day."

Lark dropped to her knee beside the dog and smoothed Nicki's thick coat. As if sensing her sadness, Nicki nudged her nose beneath Lark's arm and their gazes met. The Aussie had the most beautiful golden eyes dotted with blue. And intelligence sparkled in them.

"She likes you," Megan said.

"You sound surprised." Lark fondled Nicki's ears and the dog half shut her eyes.

"One of the reasons I've had trouble placing her is that she doesn't warm up to people. The two who took her home on a trial basis did so because of her coloring and her intelligence. They had no idea what they were getting themselves into."

What was supposed to be a twenty-minute walk

turned into half an hour. Unlike Bugsy, Nicki under-stood the concept of walking on a loose leash. She showed little interest in the tantalizing scents along the way, but kept her attention mostly on Lark. And this wasn't due to treats either, because she'd forgot-ten to grab the pouch on her way out of the shelter.

Absolutely smitten, Lark was reluctant to put Nicki back in her pen. She took out three more dogs, all with various levels of leash training, but couldn't stop thinking about the Aussie. After promising to return the following week, Lark drove home, wish-ing she'd followed her instincts and adopted the Australian shepherd.

But Megan's comments stuck in her head. A dog like Nicki needed to stay busy. She couldn't be left alone for eight hours, much less the twelve Lark worked. Granted, right now there was someone home all the time with Grace, but Lark couldn't ask Keaton to help out. And it wasn't as if he was going to be around forever. When Skye woke, she would take over responsibility for Grace and Keaton would return to his cabin. Or perhaps even the Holt ranch house.

The thought of that caused a lump to form in Lark's stomach. She'd known all along that this was a temporary situation. But knowing was different than facing the reality. Especially when she and

Keaton had been dancing around the consequences of committing to a serious relationship.

Lark drove home in a somber mood. She couldn't get Nicki's keen gaze out of her mind and couldn't shake the certainty that she and the dog had made some sort of instant connection. Surely she was simply bummed that soon Grace would leave and Keaton would have no reason to keep living with her. A dog wouldn't fill the void created by their departure, but it would keep her house from feeling empty.

Keaton was in Grace's room as Lark entered the kitchen. She could hear him talking to Grace as he fed her. Usually this would make Lark smile, but today her heart was too heavy.

Baking had always been a solution for whatever ailed her, so Lark pulled out the ingredients for a rich chocolate cake and began to measure. This particular recipe was a family favorite, something she'd always made for her father's birthday. Maybe she would take it over later. It had been over a week since she had any contact with her parents. The last conversation had been stilted and cool. Her parents were still unhappy that Keaton was helping her with Grace.

"You're home." Keaton sounded surprised as he

emerged into the great room, the bright-eyed infant cradled in his arms. "How did it go?"

"Fine." She tried to inject a light note in her voice, but wasn't completely successful.

"What happened?"

"It was just so sad. All those dogs without homes."

"You didn't have any fun?"

"Oh no. It was great. There was one dog in particular that I absolutely fell in love with."

"Have you thought about adopting a dog?"

She shook her head. "It wouldn't be fair to leave one home all day while I work. Besides, the one I liked is a trained herding dog who is used to being busy and gets destructive if left alone."

"What sort of herding?"

"Sheep and cows. Although Megan told me Nikki had worked with ducks to earn some of her titles."

Keaton looked thoughtful. "I've never worked with dogs before, but I know other ranchers who have."

This seemed like an opening. "You should meet her. She's the most amazing dog. Smart. Focused. If she's titled, I'll bet she's really well trained too."

"I'll do a little research tonight. Is she any particular breed?"

"Australian shepherd. I gather she was bred as a herding dog."

"Maybe I can go by the shelter tomorrow on my way to the ranch and meet her."

Lark was so excited she was close to bursting. "I'll let Megan know you'll be coming."

Keaton was surprised that Lark rose with him the next morning. Usually she took whatever opportunity she could to sleep after her four twelve-hour shifts. While he showered, she made coffee and a hearty breakfast of eggs, bacon and toast. He watched her while tucking away the meal. Her eyes were clear and bright. Her body hummed with energy.

She'd been even more passionate than usual the previous night. Although her innate shyness had never manifested in the bedroom, she'd taken a while to trust him completely. Last night, she'd seemed determined to smash any lingering barrier between them.

Was all this because of a dog she felt sorry for? It amused him that she was so easy to please. He'd dated women who expected expensive dinners and elaborate birthday presents. Not one of them would be delighted with a dog. It was part of Lark's charm that she was so grounded. And focused on what was truly important.

"Call later and let me know what you think after

you meet her," Lark said, following him to the door. "I don't want you to feel pressure or anything." But her eyes glowed with fervent eagerness. "I'm just really curious about your opinion."

"Sure." He slid his palm into the small of her back and pulled her close for a leisurely goodbye kiss. His heart was thumping enthusiastically by the time he lifted his lips from hers. "I'll call you when I'm headed to the ranch."

On the way to the animal shelter, Keaton caught himself humming along with the radio and shook his head in bemusement. He couldn't remember ever feeling this content. Living with Lark wasn't without its challenges, but he looked forward to coming home to her and Grace every evening, to their quiet family dinners, the passionate lovemaking after they put Grace to bed.

He liked doing whatever it took to make Lark smile. Even though he hadn't known much about her when they were kids, he suspected that she hadn't enjoyed the happiest, most carefree upbringing. It made him look for ways to bring her joy. Like going to meet the dog she'd fallen in love with. He wanted to be Lark's knight in shining armor. If that could be accomplished by rescuing Nicki, that was what he'd do.

The instant Keaton was introduced to the Australian shepherd, he understood why Lark had been so taken with her. There was a lot of intelligence in her unique parti-colored eyes and he decided, unless there were obvious temperament problems, he would bring the dog with him to the ranch to see how she got along.

"Lark really fell hard for her, didn't she?" Megan commented as Keaton stroked the dog's coat.

"She did." He was equally smitten. So much so that he was contemplating the complications that went along with co-owning the dog with her. "Lark said she's a herder. I was hoping I might be able to take her to the ranch and see how she gets along."

Megan grinned. "I've got a little paperwork for you to fill out first."

In half an hour, Keaton was on his way to the ranch. The dog curled up on the backseat of his truck for the ride as if this were just a normal day in the life. It wasn't what Keaton had expected. He figured Nicki would take a while to get used to him. As promised, he dialed Lark's cell.

"What did you think?" she asked without bothering to say hello.

"Nice dog. I've got her with me right now. We're heading to the ranch."

A long pause followed his words. "Oh."

"Megan let me take her on a trial basis," he explained. "I want to see how she is with the cows."

"If she does okay, will you adopt her?" Hope vibrated in Lark's voice.

"I thought we could discuss that over dinner tonight."

"Sure. Shoot, Grace is crying. What time will you be home?"

"Around six."

"See you then."

Keaton hung up, musing about the last time he'd included anyone in his decision making. Now it seemed that he was consulting Lark about everything from what he ate to how he spent his time. It should bother him that he had to consider someone else's opinion. In fact, he liked being half of a team. Team Grace.

Not for the first time he became aware that when her parents returned to the picture, he and Lark would have nothing more tying them together. Was this why he was considering sharing a dog with her? So they could remain in contact no matter how much pressure Tyrone and Vera put on her to cut him out of her life?

When he arrived at the ranch, Keaton's foreman gave him an odd look as he released Nicki from the truck, but one of the newer hands approached with a wide smile.

"That's a nice-looking Aussie," Treat commented, bending down to fondle the dog's head. "Where'd you get her?"

"Royal Safe Haven," Keaton explained. "Apparently she's a good herding dog. Thought I'd see how she handled herself."

He glanced down at Nicki and was surprised to see she watched him as if waiting for instructions. Keaton had half expected the dog to take off the second he let her out. Instead she glanced around, taking in the situation, and then sat at his side.

"You ever handled a herding dog before?" Treat asked.

"No, but I watched a few videos online last night and got an idea how it works."

"My uncle used to breed and train Australian shepherds. I know a little. Want me to help you out?"

Keaton glanced at his foreman. "If Jeb can spare you for an hour or so."

Jeb shrugged. "Shouldn't be a problem."

For the next thirty minutes Keaton learned the signals to guide the dog around the corral. At the end of the hour, Nicki had driven three cows into a narrow chute and Keaton was feeling pretty pleased with their teamwork. He called the dog to him and could swear she was smiling as she trotted in his direction.

"Sweet," Treat said. "She's really well trained."

"And fast," another hand said.

Keaton looked around and realized their herding exercise had drawn an audience. Jeb stood nearby. A traditionalist when it came to ranching, the old foreman wore an expression of grudging admiration.

"I can see where a few dogs like this could come in handy, especially when we're trying to move the cattle for the vet or shipping," Jeb said. "She managed them really well."

For the rest of the day wherever Keaton went, Nicki stayed within ten feet. Her eyes roamed the yard and the barns, alert and interested. By the time they headed home, Keaton knew the answer to whether Nicki was going back to Royal Safe Haven. He just wasn't sure what sort of arrangement he and Lark would come to about the dog.

When he arrived back at Lark's house, Nicki at his side, her eyes bright and alert after working cattle all day, Lark met him at the door with a cold beer and a hopeful smile.

"How'd it go?" She stood with her weight balanced on the balls of her feet, searching his expression.

"Terrific." Physically he'd been ready for Lark's enthusiastic embrace, but the strength of her jubilation sent his emotions reeling. "She's a great dog."

Lark broke off the hug and bent to love up the Aussie. "I knew you'd like her."

Keaton watched the pair with bemusement. When had making her happy begun to rule his world? "She fit in at the ranch like she'd always lived there."

"I'll bet she was happy to be working again."

"So, are you thinking about keeping her?"

He'd stopped by the pet store and bought the necessities. Food, bowls, a comfy bed for Nicki to sleep in.

"Let's see how she does with Grace."

Lark's eyes widened. "I never thought about that. She's probably never been around children, much less babies." The dog had finished wolfing down dinner and now bumped against Lark's legs. She squatted down and took Nicki's face in her hands. "What are you going to think of her? I wonder."

Grace woke shortly before dinner and Lark put her in her swing while she prepared a bottle. Keaton was in the living room, working on reports, when he heard Lark laugh. He glanced up and caught sight of the dog staring at the baby in the swing. Nicki's head was cocked in a quizzical manner, but she was completely calm. Grace was wide-awake and staring back.

"Grace is too far away to see the dog, isn't she?" Keaton asked.

"I think she can see Nicki, but maybe not perfectly."

While they watched, the Aussie nudged the swing with her nose and it moved. Grace grunted in her preemie baby way and waved her arms.

"I think they're bonding," Keaton said, setting aside his paperwork.

"Whatever they're doing, it's awfully cute."

With his heart thumping harder than normal, Keaton stared at the scene and felt a stab of envy for his absent brother. Even though Jake wasn't here to share these first few months with Grace, Keaton had no doubt that his brother would eventually show. Then it would be Skye, Jake and Grace together and both Lark and Keaton would be alone once more.

Unless Keaton took steps to keep their story from heading down that path. Lark was worth fighting for. Being with her made him happier than he'd ever been. What he needed to do was find a way to convince her they should take a shot at a relationship. And he'd better get on that fast before Skye woke up or Jake came to town, because if he waited too long, she might slip right through his fingers. And what a loss that would be.

"Keaton and I adopted a dog." Lark was sitting beside Skye's bed two days after Keaton brought Nicki home. "At least I think we both have. I'm not really sure whom Nicki actually belongs to. She's an Australian shepherd. If you've heard about the breed, you know they're really smart and good at herding." She paused. "I guess since they have shepherd as part of their name, it makes sense that they'd been good at herding."

These one-sided conversations with her sister had gotten easier in the three and a half months that Skye lay asleep. And if Lark kept up a rambling monologue, it was easier to ignore that her sister never responded.

"I know I've said it before, but I totally understand now why Holt men are so attractive. But Keaton isn't anything like Jake. He's quiet and serious. Jake was outgoing and great with people. They're as dissimilar in personalities as we are. And yet they each manage to be our perfect match."

Lark glanced around. She was keeping her voice low, but she worried that Marsha or one of her minions might overhear. The last thing she needed was for that bit of gossip to make its way around the hospital. She'd be the laughingstock of the ICU staff if they thought she had feelings for Keaton. Several times she'd made it completely clear that her relationship with Keaton was strictly about taking care of Grace.

"I think I'm falling in love with him, Skye." Lark set her forehead on her sister's hand and struggled to draw air into her tight lungs. "That makes me some kinda hypocrite, doesn't it?" With her voice muffled, she continued. "I was so awful to you when I found out you were running away with Jake. I couldn't understand how you could pick him over our family."

Four years later, Lark flushed with shame at the way she'd spoken to Skye. Lark had been convinced her sister was doing the wrong thing. She'd been smugly confident that as the older sister, she knew what was best. What would have happened to Skye if she'd listened to Lark? Grace never would've been born. Vera would have continued to hammer at Skye's spirit, criticizing every choice Skye made because it wasn't what Vera would have done.

Lark hadn't realized how much Vera had focused on Skye until she'd left town. It was once her critical eye had turned to Lark that she'd begun to understand why it hadn't been a hardship for Skye to leave her family behind.

But after such a long period with no communication, why had Skye suddenly decided to come back?

"I wish I knew something about your life these last four years. Are you still a graphic artist? Do you like your job? What was it like to discover you're pregnant and how did Jake react? I'll bet he was excited about becoming a father."

Lark paused as doubts crept in. If that was true, where was he?

"Do you have a house or an apartment? I suppose if it's the latter you're going to want to move. Grace will need a yard to run around in. Maybe even a dog. She really likes Nicki. It's funny watching them together. Nicki nudges her with her nose and Grace wriggles like crazy." The memory made her smile. "I can't wait until you wake up and can see for yourself."

Please wake up.

A familiar wave of grief swamped her, bringing a sting of tears to her eyes. In the months since Skye reappeared in Royal, Lark had been in an almost constant state of anxiety and sadness. Only in Keaton's arms did she get any relief. He had a knack for distracting her from her problems and making her exist solely in the moment.

Feeling safe was something she'd never really known before. Nor had she realized it until she'd surrendered to Keaton being in charge. The peace this brought her was temporary and addictive. Letting someone share her burden hadn't come easily, but now that she had done so, Lark was dreading being alone again.

"It's time for me to start my shift," she told Skye, clearing her throat a couple times to purge the huskiness from her voice. "I'll be back to check on you later."

"Lark?"

She jumped at the sound of her name. Turning, she spied Gloria Holt.

"Hello," she greeted. "I was just visiting my sister." Way to state the obvious. Lark's whole face felt on fire. "What brings you here?"

"Same as you."

"You're visiting Skye?"

"I try to come by at least once a week when I'm in town."

Lark shook her head. "I've never seen you before."

"I've tried not to come when I know you're working." Gloria put out her hands in a calming gesture. "Oh, that didn't come out right. What I mean is I didn't want you to be upset that I was visiting your sister."

"Why would I be?"

"There has been tension between our families for a long time."

And that tension had ruined a lot of lives.

"It's nice of you to visit Skye," Lark said. "I'm sure she appreciates the company."

Vera Taylor would have scoffed and said that Skye was unconscious and incapable of knowing that someone was nearby. Gloria Holt pulled out a book.

"I've been reading to her," she said.

"What a great idea. I've been telling her about Grace. I've heard stories where patients wake up from comas and remember conversations going on around them."

"I have a hypnosis tape I listen to as I'm falling asleep at night. It's for stress. I got it not long after the tornado came through town." Gloria grimaced. "When the ranch house was hit we lost so much that can't be replaced."

"I'm sorry to hear that, but at least no one was hurt." Lark froze as she realized she'd made another of those blunt remarks that some people took the wrong way. She hadn't meant to irritate Keaton's mother.

Fortunately Gloria took no offense. "You're absolutely right. We were more fortunate than some." Her expression clouded for a moment. "Anyway, I found that I wasn't hearing the entire recording because I was falling asleep. My hypnotherapist insisted my brain still processed the message."

"Has it helped?"

"I think so." Gloria gave her a wry smile. "I know it's having an effect on David. Despite all our losses, he's never been so calm. And he's done a great job of letting Keaton handle things."

"Your son is very determined to get things done."

Keaton's organization had impressed Lark. He worked everything on his tablet, from mind-mapping each project to formulating a process to reach his goal to tying the individual tasks to his calendar. She'd always been more comfortable doing things on paper, but after he'd shown her some of the software he used, she was beginning to see the advantages of going electronic.

"He was that way as a child. Always focused on a goal."

Lark found her curiosity aroused. She'd been in school with Jake and remembered him as a noisy, confident kid. But Keaton had been three years older and the only time he registered in her conscious thoughts was when her father complained about the *Holt* boys. "What was Keaton like as a child?"

The question surprised Gloria. "He was quiet. When he wasn't working around the ranch, he spent a lot of time reading and studying. Everything fascinated him, but math was his true passion."

"I remember that he graduated top of his class."

"When Keaton went off to college, David and I wondered if he'd want to come back to Texas and ranch. Or if he even should."

"But he came back to Royal." As she had. Lark knew she belonged here. She wondered if Keaton felt the same way or if he felt obligated to take over the family business.

"Ranching is what he wants to do." Gloria gave a "who would have guessed?" shrug.

Lark glanced at her watch. "I'd better get going. My shift starts in a little bit."

"It was nice talking to you," Gloria said.

"It was nice talking to you too." Lark gave Keaton's mom a genuine smile as she started past. "And thanks again for visiting my sister."

"She's family." Gloria's next words caught Lark by surprise. "You are too. I hope that's okay."

"Sure." What else could Lark say? Despite the animosity between their families, Lark had nothing bad to say against Gloria. Besides, with the birth of Grace, the Taylors and Holts were forever connected to each other whether any of them liked it or not. "Of course."

"Good. I know it's a lot of change for all of us,

but I hope we can set aside the past and start fresh. It's what's good for Grace, and she needs to be our top priority."

"I couldn't agree more."

Before she checked in at the nurses' station, she went to the visitors' lounge and dialed Keaton. "How are things going?"

It wasn't odd for her to check in with him, but it didn't usually happen until partway through her shift.

"Fine." His deep voice was steady and reassuring. A life preserver for her to cling to. "Are you okay?" His perceptiveness never ceased to amaze her.

"Everything's fine. Nothing has changed with Skye. I told her about Nicki and how cute she and Grace are together." What she should tell him was how hearing his voice calmed her. But he probably already suspected that. "I'm getting ready to start my shift and wasn't sure I'd have the chance to call before you went to bed."

"You didn't answer my question. How are you?"

"Sad. Skye's been in her coma so long. I'm worried that she might not ever wake." There. She'd said it. This was where she needed him to reassure her that everything would be okay.

"I know it's hard, but you need to stay strong. Skye will come out of this just fine."

Lark's shoulders sagged. "Thank you."

"No need for that. I'm not just here for Grace. I care about you and I know how stressed you've been." The deep note of concern in his tone was exactly what she needed to rally. "Why don't you call me as you're leaving the hospital? I'll have a hot bath and a cup of tea waiting."

She'd never lived with a man before, but she knew Keaton's thoughtfulness wasn't the norm. "You know I like coming home to you, right?"

"I'm glad because I like coming home to you, as well."

Silence followed their mutual confessions.

"And you know there's room enough for two in my tub."

"Won't you be too tired?"

"To take a hot bath with you?" She chuckled, feeling much better than she had ten minutes ago. "Never."

Eleven

Keaton cradled Lark's left foot in his hand and pressed his thumb into her arch. The low moan she made was almost sexual and caused his temperature to climb.

"That's amazing," she murmured, her head thrown back, eyes closed.

The water lapped against her chest, pushing a crest of bubbles almost to her throat. It was a little after nine in the evening. As promised, Keaton had drawn her a bath for her arrival home, but before she could slide into the heated water, she'd fallen upon him with determined vigor. They'd made love in slow, silent appreciation of each other and the passion between them.

Her bath had cooled by the time sweat coated their

bodies, but lovemaking had done more to relax her than a dozen hours of soaking in hot water. Later, she'd watched him from the doorway that separated bedroom and bathroom, her eyes lazy with contentment as he emptied and refilled the tub. Naked and completely at home in her skin, she bore little resemblance to the shy, self-contained woman she became outside her home. A tigress lurked beneath her skin. He loved being the only one who got to feel her claws.

"My parents came by today to see Grace and have dinner," he remarked, switching his attention to her other foot. "Mom made her famous lasagna. There's leftovers if you're interested."

"As much as I've been dying to try your mom's lasagna," Lark said. "I'm way too comfortable to move at the moment."

The sound of her cell phone came from her bedroom. Keaton recognized the caller because Lark had set Carly Simon's "*You're So Vain*" as her mother's ring tone. There was little love lost between mother and daughter, yet Lark remained unwilling to make waves with her parents.

"She's been calling me for the last three days." Lark's huge sigh spoke volumes. "I'm guessing she or my dad heard that you and I showed up at the

Richardson party together and she wants to tell me how stupid I am for associating with you."

"You haven't spoken with her yet?"

"Why bother when I know what she's going to say?"

The support Keaton wanted to offer would only cause Lark more grief with her parents. This was a battle she had to face on her own, and that frustrated him.

"My parents found a condo they like on the beach in Gulf Shores, Alabama, and put in an offer. It's on the tenth floor and has great views." Keaton couldn't imagine his active father settling into beach life, but his mother had been thrilled by the four bedrooms. "I guess each floor is a single unit, and there are three-hundred-and-sixty-degree views."

The conversation was mundane enough to allow Lark to relax. "Sounds fantastic, but it's a long way from here."

"My mother has always been fond of the beach."

"What about your dad?"

"He likes making my mom happy. Says he's going to work harder on his golf game." In the years since Keaton took over supervision of the ranch business, David Holt had begun playing a round or two a week. "And they have friends that bought in the same building several years ago."

"Is this a full-time move?"

"At this point I don't think so." Keaton recalled his mother's glowing descriptions of the town and the unit. "But I think they were leaning that way before the tornado hit."

Of course, that was before Skye had shown up and Grace had been born. Lark picked up his train of thought.

"We don't know that anything has changed really. Jake hasn't shown up yet and there's no reason to believe Skye has any intention of staying in Royal."

"My mother is afraid that she's never going to see Grace again after Jake and Skye take over as parents."

Lark looked worried. "Surely the fact that Skye was coming back to Royal is a good indication that she was ending four years of silence."

"Is that what you think?"

"Why else?"

"It still bothers me that she was alone." Keaton turned his attention toward the baby monitor set up on the sink. A faint cry rose from the speaker. "That she didn't contact anyone and let them know she was coming."

They both stopped speaking when they heard another cry. Sometimes Grace made noises in her sleep and then subsided. In silence they waited to determine what would happen next. It was quiet for several seconds, so Keaton spoke again.

"You'd think she'd want Jake with her when she came to tell everyone she was pregnant."

"Or maybe that would have made things so much worse?" Lark sighed. They'd speculated on every sort of scenario and hadn't settled on a single one.

Another cry pierced the silence. This time both adults jumped into action. Keaton waved Lark back into the water as he stood and grabbed a towel.

"I'll get her. Stay and relax."

She shook her head. "I'm already feeling like a prune. Besides, I should probably call my mother back."

Water ran down her body as she stood. Soap bubbles clung to her nipples and dotted her midsection and thighs. Keaton stared at her in absolute fascination, only half-aware that Grace's unhappiness was escalating.

"Keaton?" Lark caught him staring at her as she turned from releasing the tub drain.

"Have I mentioned how gorgeous you are?"

Her face, already flushed from the hot water, grew even rosier. "Several times today." She let her gaze rake down his body in slow deliberation. "And right back at you. I'm not sure I'd ever get tired of looking at you."

"We should institute naked Sundays."

Seeing he was completely serious, she laughed. "It's January."

"True."

Instead of handing her the towel she pointed to, he wrapped it around her. The kiss he gave her was hard and quick. Mostly he'd wanted a second to enjoy the softness of her breasts crushed against his chest. He kept his hands away from any naked skin. Touching her silky wet skin would only delay getting to Grace.

"I guess I can wait until it warms up in April." And with a provocative pat on her towel-clad backside, he exited the bathroom.

Lark stared at Keaton's retreating form while his words played over and over in her mind. April? He was thinking they would still be living together three months from now? Surely he didn't believe that Skye would still be in a coma or Jake would continue to be missing. That meant he expected to still be together even after they no longer had Grace's welfare to look after.

A shiver raised goose bumps on her arms. She grabbed a quick shower and washed her hair, then dressed in a pair of her new silky pajamas. Keaton enjoyed running his hands over the slippery material, and she adored having every inch of her curves caressed by him. The thought made her smile. Even though her desire had been sated by their earlier lovemaking, it took very little to rouse the ache between her thighs.

Telling her body to behave, Lark headed into the kitchen to find Gloria's lasagna and open a bottle of red wine. Another perk of having Keaton living with her was that she'd learned to appreciate the finer vintages. Luckily the Holts' wine cellar hadn't been damaged during the storm and he enjoyed sharing his favorites with her.

While she heated up the lasagna, she kept one ear tuned to the nursery. Grace had calmed. Keaton certainly had the magic touch with her. The baby had probably woken wet or messy. She was very particular where her diaper was concerned. Someday she'd probably be equally determined about her fashion. Something that might make her acceptable to her grandmother.

From the time Skye was a toddler, she'd been thrust onto the pageant circuit by their mother, whose obsession with appearance and winning had been extreme. Lark remembered visiting Skye's room when she and their mother were gone for the weekend and trying on her sister's massive crowns or whatever sequined, tulle-enriched dress had been left behind. There'd been dozens in Skye's closet, some of them for the pageants that required specialty routines.

One time her father had caught her and paddled her backside hard. She wasn't sure which had hurt more, the spanking or his disappointment. Fortunately he'd kept the tale from his wife or Lark might have been punished worse than she had. In later years, when she'd begun to understand the value of things, she'd discovered those silly, overembellished dresses cost between five hundred and a thousand dollars apiece.

Keaton carried a very wide-awake Grace to the infant gym and laid her beneath the arches. He then joined Lark in the kitchen, where she offered him a lingering kiss. The microwave dinged before they got too carried away and Lark fetched her dinner. She decided to break her rule against eating on the sofa so she could join Keaton while he watched another one of those educational shows he'd introduced her to.

As they sat in companionable silence, attention alternating between the enormous television and their niece happily batting at the animals suspended above her, Lark decided not to broach the question tickling her since Keaton had teased her about naked Sundays. Instead she let herself enjoy the weight of his hand on her thigh and the familiar jump in her pulse as he kissed her neck and shoulder during the commercial breaks.

At long last, nerves mellowed by Keaton's solid presence, a delicious meal and two glasses of wine, Lark called her mother. Keaton offered to leave the room, but she needed his strength beside her. With her arm linked with his, she waited for her mother to pick up. By the fifth ring Lark was convinced there would be no answer and had moved her thumb to end the call when she heard her mother's voice.

"Yes?"

"Hello, Mother. It's Lark. I was just returning your call."

"It's about time. I've left you five messages."

Lark hadn't realized that. She avoided looking at her phone log since her mother had begun calling. "Sorry." She had no excuse. "What's so urgent?"

"Haven't you listened to any of my messages?"

"No."

"That's very inconsiderate. What if something had happened to your father?"

"Has it?"

"No."

"Then what's the problem?" The question came out a little more bluntly than she'd intended.

She'd had no contact with her parents since the

little incident outside the ICU, and the silence had been nice. Immediately guilt lashed at her. This was her mother. As little as they got along, Lark owed her respect. Or if that wasn't possible, civility.

"The problem is I was ambushed at the beauty shop about you and that Holt."

Lark wasn't sure what to say so she kept silent.

"Are you *involved* with him?" Vera made the word *involved* sound like a mortal sin.

"He's helping me take care of Grace. You knew that."

"You didn't tell us that he'd also moved in."

While it was on the tip of her tongue to snap that she was twenty-seven years old and perfectly within her rights to do whatever she wanted with the house she'd bought, Lark knew that her mother would never hear the logic of that.

"It's made things much easier."

"Are you sleeping with him?"

Keaton's fingers moved between hers in a soothing caress. This was the moment she'd been dreading since her feelings for Keaton had begun to surface. She would be forced to choose between her parents and the man she was falling in love with.

"The feud between the Taylors and the Holts isn't my fight," she said, admitting nothing. "I'm sick of being caught in the middle of it."

"You are." Her mother gasped, assuming the worst from Lark's lack of swift and immediate denial. "Your father will be devastated."

"Keaton is an honorable man. He cares about Grace and about me."

"He's using you," her mother spat. "You're nothing but a convenience."

Even knowing how vehemently her parents hated the Holts, it still shocked Lark that they would turn so completely against her. Was this what Skye had experienced? And then Lark had gone and heaped more disapproval on her sister's slender shoulders. Shame rose to choke her.

"I'm sorry you feel that way, Mother," Lark said, forcing her voice to remain steady. "I have to go." And without giving her mother another opportunity to spew more negativity, she hung up.

Keaton's arms came around her and pulled her tight to his chest. His lips drifted over her cheek toward her ear. "I'm sorry you had to go through that."

His solidness absorbed the tremors that racked her body. "She can't understand."

"She doesn't care about your happiness," he said as he ran his hands up and down her spine. "Or Skye's. Neither of them does."

To her relief, he didn't ask her why she hadn't admitted to being involved with him, but had let her mother draw her own conclusions. Lark felt as if she'd betrayed him, been disloyal to the relationship developing between them. If she truly was falling in love with him, why hadn't she proudly claimed him?

"It's been a really long day." Lark looked at the baby. Grace was showing no signs of fading. "If it's okay with you, I think I'm going to turn in."

"Sure. Grace and I will watch a little basketball. You get some sleep."

With a nod, Lark left the couch and washed her plate and wineglass. Nicki chose to follow her into the bedroom. As the Aussie curled up on her bed, Lark slid between the cool covers and lay shivering. Although she'd been truthful about being tired, sleep was a long way away. Now that her parents knew she and Keaton were together, how long would it be before they started issuing ultimatums and forced her to choose between them and Keaton?

Worse, Lark wasn't sure whom she'd pick. Even though she wasn't their favorite, she was still their daughter. Outside of Skye they were the only family she had, and Lark had no idea what sort of relationship she'd have with her sister when Skye woke up. They hadn't spoken in four years. Wasn't that a pretty good indication that Lark hadn't been forgiven?

Keaton had given her no direct indication just how

deep his feelings for her ran. What if she chose him only to find out he wanted little beyond great sex and companionship? His parents weren't as rigid as hers, but she suspected they weren't wild that Keaton was with her. From what Skye had told her before she left, they'd been furious to learn about her romance with their son. Their anger had driven Jake from Royal. He'd been the one who persuaded Skye to leave.

That wouldn't happen with her and Keaton. He was tied to the ranch. They would be forced to stick around and bear the brunt of their parents' vehement disapproval. Lark almost choked on a ragged exhalation. Keaton might be strong enough to cope, but was she? And what damage would it do to their relationship? In the end the Taylor/Holt feud would tear them apart.

When Keaton came to bed an hour or so later, Lark rolled toward him and pressed against him from breast to thigh. He claimed her mouth without hesitation and made love to her with fierce passion. She left her mark on him, her fingernails scoring his back as she climaxed. Keaton followed her seconds later with a powerful orgasm of his own.

No words passed between them as they lay gasping for breath. As soon as they'd sufficiently recovered, Keaton shifted her into the perfect niche at his side and smoothed her sweat-damp hair off her face. Lark snuggled her nose into his neck and breathed his unique musk. Exhausted from her long day and their vigorous lovemaking, she resisted sleep. How many more nights would she have him like this?

"Go to sleep," he murmured as if sensing her mind's restlessness. "There's nothing you can do about anything at the moment."

She lifted her head for his kiss and smiled beneath his lips. Only a very foolish woman would push this man out of her life because she was too afraid to upset her family. And Lark was many things, but she'd never been called foolish.

Keaton neared the ruins of the town hall, his thoughts far from the task ahead. After a great deal of deliberation and consultation with the construction contractor, a plan had been created for recovering the city's records. In the weeks leading up to today, much of the rubble had been cleared from the site. Today, the tarp that had been thrown over the records storage area was gone and heavy machinery stood at the ready to begin the delicate task of lifting the large chunks of concrete off the sturdy filing cabinets that held the town's records.

"I guess we were lucky that someone had the foresight to move everything into fireproof cabinets,"

Stella Daniels commented as Keaton approached. The acting mayor was no longer the nondescript town hall administrative assistant she once was. In the months since the tornado had landed Richard Vance, Royal's major, in the hospital, she'd blossomed into a stunning woman who'd taken charge during the crisis and performed brilliantly. "Fireproofing means more than just heat resistant, you know."

"When I first got started on this project, I did a little research," Keaton admitted. "They're waterproof and designed to survive short falls. As long as nothing too heavy landed on them, we should find the cabinets intact."

Stella eyed him. "I just knew you were the right man to take on this job."

"This town has given a lot to the Holt family," he said, tugging on the brim of his cowboy hat. "I'm happy I can pitch in and help."

Which was true. Although he participated in very few social activities around town, Keaton's problem-solving abilities had been unanimously welcomed. He'd been surprised how quickly he was caught up in the community spirit. Helping where he could, he'd been involved with over a dozen repair or cleanup projects. But except for a few simple construction jobs like the Richardsons' barn, he left the major rebuilding to the experts.

"I see the crews are assembled," Stella said. "Shall we get started?"

The delicate process of removing concrete from the area where the records room had once been was tedious and slow. In addition to the large chunks of building material, there were several yards of pulverized debris that had once been walls and ceiling to sift through. It was late afternoon when there was enough cleared away to begin the removal of the files.

Moving carefully through the rubble, Keaton inspected each of the cabinets before they were hauled away and was pleased that despite the dents to the metal caused by the building's collapse, the contents were intact and mostly undisturbed.

In addition to the modern files, there were several antique cabinets that no one had ever bothered to remove. These had not fared as well. Keaton thought there might have been four or five of them on the far side of the room. It was hard to tell an exact number, as they had mostly been reduced to kindling.

One cabinet had fared better than the others. Although one side had been crushed, the other had six drawers still intact. He pulled out one of the drawers, surprised that it rolled smoothly, and noted that it was empty. Keaton felt foolish as he investigated the other five drawers in the same way. Did he really expect to find some lost piece of paperwork that proved his family were the true owners of the two thousand acres of lakes and superb pasture now part of the Taylors' ranch?

Stella, accompanied by her fiancé, Aaron Nichols, had stopped by to see how the work was going. They were picking their way toward Keaton.

"You've made amazing progress," Stella said, stepping around a small pile of twisted metal that had once been a light and stopping beside Keaton. "How amazing that part of this cabinet looks unscathed while the rest of it is destroyed."

"As are three or four others." Keaton gestured at the other cabinets.

"Was there anything in it?" She pulled out a drawer the same way he had.

"No. I'm guessing they were original to the building, but no one bothered to get rid of them when the fireproof ones were brought in."

"They look old enough to have been worth something before the tornado struck."

The cleanup crew had been steadily working in their direction, and now they began to toss bits of the shattered cabinets into the bucket of the loader idling nearby. While Keaton gave Stella an update on the progress made that day, the loader moved off to empty its bucket into the nearby construction dumpster. When it returned, Keaton and Aaron stepped to opposite sides of the mostly intact cabinet and picked it up.

They'd shifted it several feet when Stella called out, "Wait! There's something caught underneath it."

Keaton glanced in her direction as she ducked down and came up with a yellowed piece of paper. "Is that it?"

"I think so."

He and Aaron finished moving the cabinet to the loader, checking for more loose paper before returning to Stella. They found her studying the document with interest.

"What is it?" Aaron asked, peering over Stella's shoulder at the paper she held.

"Looks like a bill of sale for some land back in 1880." Her gaze shifted to Keaton. "Is Edwin Holt any relation?"

Something about the way she asked the question made Keaton's heart thunder in his chest. "My great grandfather many times over."

"Good thing we found it. I think it's the bill of sale for your land."

"My family settled here in the 1860s."

"Are you sure?"

Keaton nodded. "Edwin Holt came here not long after the Civil War ended."

"Maybe they didn't buy your family's ranch until much later. Take a look."

But even as Stella held out the document, Keaton knew what he'd see. And yet it seemed impossible. All the times he'd hope the bill of sale would be rediscovered had been little more than wishful thinking.

He stripped off his gloves in order to handle the aged paper with utmost care. With his thoughts a chaotic swirl he had a hard time discerning the words. After blinking a few times, the thin, spidery script began to make sense. He grew lightheaded at what he read.

"What is it?" Aaron pressed, as the silence dragged on.

Keaton lifted his gaze from the document, scarcely believing what he'd seen, mind reeling at the implications. "I think it might be the missing document that started the feud between my family and the Taylors."

And the basis for a new cycle of conflict between the families.

Twelve

Lark rubbed her eyes and yawned. At three in the morning, the ICU was relatively peaceful. Machines beeped and whirred, keeping their patients alive. Once again Marsha had called in to say she couldn't make it, so Lark had agreed to stay on a few extra hours. How much longer was the senior nurse going to tolerate this? By Lark's estimate, Marsha was out for one reason or another three or four times a month. Marsha had probably gotten away with it this long because of the way she made her boss feel sorry for her.

"How are things going?"

Turning, she spotted Becky Jones, the head nurse in charge of ICU. "Fine. It was a quiet day, which is turning into a peaceful night."

"You look half-dead on your feet."

"Grace had a hard time settling down after her feeding last night and I missed a few hours of sleep."

Even though it had been Keaton's night to get up with Grace, she'd been so miserable that she and Keaton had taken turns trying to calm her. In the end it was Nicki who'd convinced the baby to settle down by gently nudging her until Grace stopped crying. After two hours of frantic crying, the abrupt quiet had been nothing short of amazing.

Becky smiled in sympathy. "I remember my two at that age. I swore there was some magic switch that flipped on in them as soon as the sun went down." She shook her head. "The good news is it won't last long. Pretty soon she'll be sleeping through the night."

"I hope so."

"Judy should be back from her break in a couple minutes," Becky said. "Why don't you go sit with Skye for a while? I can handle things here."

"Thanks."

"No, I should be thanking you. It's been great having you here in the ICU. I'm going to miss you when you go back to surgery."

Lark smiled at the compliment. Becky wasn't usually one to hand out praise. "It was nice of you to let me transfer into your department so I could stay close to my sister."

"She needed you. And it turns out we needed you, as well. Our efficiency has gone up dramatically thanks to you."

"I didn't do much, just saw a few places where our processes varied and pointed them out. You were the one who implemented the changes."

"I know that hasn't made you popular among some of your fellow nurses."

Lark shrugged and tried to keep her expression as neutral as possible. "I can be a little forthright. It's gotten me into trouble in the past."

"I see it as speaking your mind for the good of the department. And you didn't say anything that wasn't true." Becky's lips tightened. "Not everyone can face that there's always room for improvement."

Was she speaking of Marsha? From what Lark gathered, Marsha's absences had escalated since the tornado hit Royal. She'd been on duty that day and not far from the west wing when it collapsed. She hadn't been hurt, but it was possible that she was suffering from PTSD.

"Change can be hard," Lark said. "Especially when it originates from a know-it-all newcomer."

Becky gave a light laugh. "Go sit with Skye. Talk

to her about Grace. Maybe if she knows her baby needs her she'll wake up."

"Good idea."

Lark didn't tell her boss that she'd already been doing that. She drew up a chair beside her sister's bed and took Skye's hand. For a while she didn't know how to begin. Then she began as she always did and let her words flow from there.

"Grace is thriving. I swear if you stare at her long enough, you can see her grow. I don't know if you recall that we have a dog now. Nicki has turned out to be a terrific addition to the family." Lark paused and swallowed the lump in her throat. "Keaton bought this wrap thing that I wear when Grace wants to be held and I need to keep my hands free. On the warmer days I put Grace in it and take Nicki for a walk. I swear since I've started doing that she's doubled her formula consumption. I think the fresh air is good for her."

While she talked, Lark stared at the monitors that surrounded her sister's bed. They registered all Skye's vitals, their beeps and flashing numbers soothing.

"Mom's been calling. She found out that Keaton and I had gone to the party at the Richardsons' together. She guessed that Keaton and I are sleeping together. I don't need to tell you how angry she is.

I haven't spoken to Dad. I don't imagine he'll want to have anything to do with me now that I've gone over to the dark side." Bitter amusement darkened her tone. "I know I've said it plenty already, but I'm sorry. I really screwed up when I found out you were leaving Royal with Jake. I didn't appreciate then how hard our parents were on you or how painful it must have been to have to choose between him and us."

Lost in her misery, Lark barely noticed the minute pressure against her hand. But she saw Skye's finger twitch. Too scared to blink lest she missed it again, Lark stared at her sister's pale hand and willed it to move again. Nothing happened.

"The difference between Keaton and Jake, though," she continued, hoping that maybe something she'd been saying had reached her sister, "is that while Jake loved you with all his heart, I'm not sure if Keaton's thinking of forever and me in the same sentence." Still no movement from Skye, so Lark kept going. "Mom told me he's using me. She's convinced that as soon as we're no longer taking care of Grace, he'll head back to the Holt Ranch and never give me another thought."

The pain her mother's words had caused was reflected in Lark's voice, but it all vanished in an instant when Skye's fingers moved again, more obviously this time. Maybe all this time Lark had been using the wrong stimuli to reach her sister.

"It hasn't happened yet, but they're going to make me choose. The same way they made you choose. I'm not as strong as you. I'm worried that I'll end things with Keaton, but that Mom and Dad still won't want me as their daughter."

Another pulse came from Skye's hand. This one stronger than ever.

"You're waking up," Lark exclaimed, dropping her head over her sister's hand. "You're finally waking up." And as pain tore through her chest, she began to cry.

At six in the morning, Keaton was awake and troubled over the empty bed beside him. Lark should have been home a little after midnight. Something was wrong. He bolted up and reached for his phone. Nicki leaped to her feet and came over to nudge his hip with her nose. He absently stroked the Aussie's head as he checked for messages.

A three-word text explained where she was. Skye's waking up.

He was in the middle of responding when he heard the garage door and slid out of bed. He met Lark just inside the door between the kitchen and the garage. Without a word, he threw his arms around her and spun her off her feet. Nicki frolicked around them, animated by their excitement.

"I just got your text," he explained, setting her on her feet so he could frame her face with his hands and survey her expression. "How is she?"

"She only came to for a couple seconds, but it was fantastic. Her doctor told me she'll go back and forth between conscious and unconscious for a while with the periods of consciousness growing with time."

"This is fantastic news." News he longed to be able to share with Jake. Not wanting to dampen Lark's euphoria, Keaton pushed his annoyance aside. This was a time to celebrate. "Do they have any idea how long her recovery will take?"

Lark shook her head. "It's too early to tell." She leaned her head against his chest, wrapped her arms around his waist and squeezed tight. "It's going to be all right."

"I never doubted it."

Keaton set his cheek against her soft hair and pushed his own news to the back of his mind. This was not the time to tell her about the documents he'd found in the wreckage of the town hall. And until his lawyer was able to verify their validity, there was no reason to stir up trouble. That was why he hadn't told his mother. She'd feel obligated to tell her husband, and Keaton's father would waste no time confronting Tyrone Taylor. Keaton wanted to handle the delicate situation with Lark before the news got to her father.

"Is it okay if I grab a couple hours of sleep? I wasn't sure what your plans were this morning."

"I'm supposed to be back at the town hall around nine. Do you want me to call my mom again and see if she can come by?"

"No. I'll be fine with a quick nap. I'm used to sleeping when I can, so I'll grab naps while Grace sleeps."

With the way her eyes were sparkling, Keaton wondered if she'd sleep at all. "Are you sure you don't want to go back to the hospital and sit with Skye after you get some sleep?"

"She's in good hands and it will take a while before she'll be coherent enough for conversation. I'll go check on her tonight. If anything happens between now and then, the hospital will call me."

"And you'll call my mother?"

"Definitely."

They grabbed a leisurely shower together and Keaton felt Lark's muscles loosen beneath his hands. As tempted as he was by her soft murmurs of pleasure and the skimming of her palms over his own soapy flesh, Keaton tucked her into bed without exhausting her further. She was fast asleep before he dressed and left the room.

Grace lay awake in her crib, her eyes fixed on the mobile above her. Unlike her father, she tended to wake happy in the morning. Keaton recalled Jake dragging himself blurry-eyed to school every morning.

"Good morning, sunshine," he crooned, lifting her into his arms. She blinked at him, her blue eyes not quite able to focus. "Your auntie Lark has come home with great news. Your mother has come out of her coma and she will be so excited to meet you."

Keaton wondered how long before mother and child were reunited. He hoped for Grace's sake it was soon. Although he and Lark had done a good job, Grace needed her mother. And her father.

As promised, Lark woke in two hours and took charge of Grace so Keaton could get back to the town hall. Between feeding, burping, changing and a stint in the infant gym, Grace was ready to go back to sleep.

Lark put the baby down, kissed Keaton on the chin and shuffled off to the bedroom once more. She was half-asleep; her extra-long shift and the excitement over her sister's recovery had drained her. Keaton wanted to stay home and watch over both her and Grace. With Skye awakening from the coma, his time with the pair was growing short and he hated the empty hollow in his chest at the thought.

There was nothing he could do about losing Grace. She belonged with her mother. But preventing Lark from slipping from his life was something he could control. The previous day's discovery gnawed at him. As close as he and Lark had grown these last several weeks, there was no question in his mind that the revelation of the misplaced bill of sale would put a strain on his relationship with Lark if she sided with her father on the issue.

He might just lose her forever.

Yet he owed it to his family to fight for the land the Taylor family currently claimed. They needed the lakes on the disputed property to keep their cattle fed. Because of the water, this area was abundant with grass. They could shift the herds until they could complete repairs on the damage the tornado had done to the system they used to irrigate their current pastures and buy more lightweight calves to increase their herd.

Keaton realized the implications of the choice he had to make. Jake had prioritized love over family. Keaton had no idea if his brother was happy with his decision, but if he had to guess, he'd say the answer was yes.

But Keaton had never been one to lead with his heart. He acted based on facts and logic. Choosing a technical approach to the cattle business, he'd altered the type of grass in the pastures and set up irrigation. The plentiful, high-quality forage allowed them to double the number of cattle per acre. This had enabled the ranch to become wildly profitable.

Logic told him to do what was good for his family and the ranch. He and Lark had known each other for less than a month. They'd been involved for two weeks. No matter how intense the chemistry between them and how much his heart ached when she snuggled against him, was he really ready to choose something as intangible as love over something that would benefit his family for decades to come?

The answer was very clear.

Lark sat in the chair beside her sister's bed and reached for her hand. From what Jessa and Ivy had told her, Skye had awakened twice since Lark left the hospital earlier. Both times, she'd only been conscious for a few minutes, but she knew her name and although she seemed surprised to be at Royal Memorial Hospital, she recognized the town she grew up in.

"Your baby is eager to be held by her mommy," Lark said, willing Skye to open her eyes. "The sooner you start getting better, the faster you two will be reunited."

A tall man in white approached the bed. "How's our patient today? I heard she's woken up quite a few times."

The smile Dr. Lucas Wakefield sent Lark's way was supposed to fill her with encouragement. The handsome, accomplished surgeon oozed confidence in the operating room where he excelled, and at a patient's bedside. It was hard to feel anxious when he was around.

"Yes," Lark said. "I can finally breathe again."

"I know this has been very hard on you," Dr. Wakefield said. "And I hope you realize that she has a long recovery ahead of her. There will be physical therapy and it sounds like she may have gaps in her memory."

"There's more than you're saying." Lark braced herself. "What else are you worried about?"

"She might have trouble doing everyday functions. The memory loss may be extensive and permanent."

"You're trying to say she may not be back to a hundred percent."

"We'll know more as she stabilizes and begins to respond to stimuli."

Ever a pragmatist, Lark struggled against being

swallowed by anxiety. Dr. Wakefield was simply trying to prepare her. She briefly closed her eyes and longed for the support of Keaton's strong arms.

"Thank you for everything you've done," Lark said. "I know my sister wouldn't have survived without your skill."

Dr. Wakefield smiled. "Thank you. I'll check back in later."

Left on her own once more, Lark fought back tears and tried to remember a time when her emotions had run away with her like this. Falling in love with Keaton had brought her feelings into sharp focus.

"Lark?" Skye's voice sounded blurry and far away.

"Skye." She stood up and leaned over her sister. Brushing her fingers against Skye's pale face, she met her sister's green eyes and smiled. "I'm so glad you're awake."

"I'm in the hospital."

At least her short-term memory was okay. "Do you know how we can get a hold of Jake?"

"Where is he?" Skye's gaze searched past Lark. Panic tightened her face. "I need him."

"I know." Lark fought to keep her voice calm and soothing. "Do you have his cell number?"

"Phone." Her lids drooped, voice fading.

"Your phone is gone." But it was too late. Skye was out once more.

Lark suspected that her sister would have no idea what Jake's number was. She'd probably programmed it into her missing phone and never given it another thought. But if she remembered her own number, then perhaps they could get a hold of a bill and Jake's number should be on it.

But that wasn't going to happen soon, and Lark settled back to wait for her sister to return to consciousness.

Keaton paced his lawyer's office. The document had been authenticated, but the battle was far from over.

"It could take months before the courts agree that the land belongs to your family," Sean Abbot said, "and that's if the Taylors don't decide to tie things up with a counterclaim."

If that happened, the battle was going to be ugly, and the one who would suffer would be Lark. Skye was waking up. She would contact Jake and the two of them would spirit Grace off, perhaps never to return again. Keaton's heart lurched at the thought.

"Any idea how to keep that from happening?"

Sean had been the Holts' lawyer for the last twenty years. He'd been involved in every lawsuit and countersuit that the two families had thrown at each other.

"I've heard you've been staying with Lark and helping her out with your niece. Does she have any pull with Tyrone? Maybe if she spoke to him."

Keaton shook his head. "Even if I thought it would help, I'd never ask her to do that. This is my battle with Taylor."

"Well," Sean said, his expression somber, "that's what it's going to be. A battle. Do you want me to get the court documents started?"

Keaton hesitated before answering. He picked up the envelope with a copy of the bill of sale. "I'll call you in a couple hours." Before he moved forward, he had to tell Lark and then her father.

He wasn't looking forward to either conversation. Lark deserved to know before anything happened, but she was preoccupied with her sister's recovery and didn't need to be worried about how the discovery of the lost document was going to impact her family. She'd probably insist on going with him to confront her father.

Tyrone was going to rant and threaten and end up taking his frustration out on Lark because he would view her as a traitor for suggesting they try for an amicable solution.

She was at home when he called looking for her.

This relieved him. He wouldn't have told her at the hospital where her reaction might have been noticed by her coworkers. The twenty-minute drive gave him plenty of time to prepare the best strategy for approaching the subject of the long-lost bill of sale. He hoped that she'd be sensible when she found out he intended to take the land back.

The woman who greeted him at the door wasn't the bubbly, optimistic woman who'd headed for the hospital earlier that day. She threw herself into his arms and clung as if he was the only thing keeping her safe.

"What's wrong?" he murmured against her hair, wondering if something had happened to Skye. "Is your sister okay?"

Lark pushed out of his arms and ran her fingers under her eyes to scoop up the moisture. "I'm such a mess."

"You're beautiful." He cupped her cheek in his palm and leaned down to kiss her. His heart thumped against his ribs as she yielded beneath his lips. Before the chemistry between them flared, he broke off the kiss and drew her toward the couch in the great room. "Tell me what's going on."

"Dr. Wakefield came to see Skye today while I was there. He's concerned about her memory and warned me she may never be back one hundred percent."

Keaton had done some reading on head trauma and knew the recovery was slow and sometimes not complete. He hadn't said anything to Lark about it, figuring as a medical professional she already knew the odds and didn't need him heaping worry on her.

"But she's young and strong. And she has a beautiful baby girl to motivate her."

They sat down on the couch and Lark made a move to kiss him. Keaton drew back and she regarded him in confusion. Now it was her turn to ask what was wrong.

"While moving the records at the town hall, I made a discovery." He began his tale in gentle tones, knowing what was to come would be jarring.

"What sort of discovery?"

"An old bill of sale that's been lost for years."

She stared at his face, and her expression froze. "The one our families have been battling over for years?"

"That's the one. It was behind one of the antique filing cabinets in the records room."

"Rather convenient that *you* found it," she said, her tone flat.

"It's not a forgery if that's what you're implying. It's been authenticated." In his rush to avert her suspicions, he didn't consider the conclusions she'd draw from that.

She shifted away from him. "How long ago did you find it?"

"A few days."

"Days?" She looked stricken. "How many?"

"I found it the day Skye woke up for the first time."

"We've been together a bunch of times since then." She scurried off the couch. "We...we made love. You should have told me. I deserved to know."

"You were worried about Skye. I didn't want to distract you."

She clenched her hands into fists. "Distract me? Seems more like you wanted to deceive me. I trusted you."

"You still can." Keaton stood. Had he subconsciously known her deep-seated distrust of his family would overwhelm any faith she'd placed in him? Was that why he'd waited so long to tell her? "I didn't want to upset you unnecessarily if the document wasn't valid."

"What are you planning to do?"

"The land belongs to Holt Ranch."

"So you're going to just take it?"

"It's not like that. The land isn't yours."

"You can't just take it back. My family needs

those lakes to irrigate our tree farm and water our cattle."

He tried to assume a placating tone. "If your father would see reason for a change and work with me, we could offer him a water lease." It was more generous than Tyrone Taylor had ever been with the Holts.

"You intend to charge us for what's been ours for decades?"

So it was *us* now. After how her parents had treated Lark. The way they'd refused to help with Grace. Their abandonment of Skye as she lay in her hospital bed fighting for her life.

His anger with her parents, specifically her father, boiled over. "It's Holt land."

Immediately he knew he'd chosen the wrong tack. She looked as if he'd slapped her.

"We'll fight you." Her voice quivered with dismay. "With everything we have."

"Lark, be reasonable. Let's talk about this."

"Reasonable?" The word carried the weight of all her distress. "Why do I have to be reasonable? My father was right about you. You Holts will do anything to get what you want." Her breath caught. "Even sleep with me."

Her accusation struck him like a whip. "You can't really think that."

"My mother said you were using me. She was right."

"That's not true. I only wanted to help you with Grace."

"You did a little bit more than that." She spoke the words as if they tasted bitter.

"You're right," he said, all passion leaving his voice. "I also fell in love with you."

Thirteen

He was lying. Lark stared at Keaton in horror. The room around her grew fuzzy, but his face remained crystal clear. How had she been so stupid? She'd actually believed that he cared about her when all along he was manipulating her emotions so that she'd turn against her family.

One part of her brain reminded her that the discovery of the missing document had only recently happened and they'd been intimate for weeks. He knew she had no ability to sway her father. Skye was the sister who wrapped their father around her little finger.

"You don't love me," she said, the denial struggling to escape her tight throat. "We barely know each other. No one falls in love that fast." But hadn't she? Could she honestly deny that she loved him with her whole heart? "You just want me on your side against my father."

"I want you *by* my side, but only because in the last few weeks you've become my world."

He looked so earnest. Believable. "Then can't you forget you found the bill of sale?" In her heart she knew it was unfair to ask him.

"I don't want to lose you." He closed his eyes and his face turned to granite. When he met her gaze once more, his expression was bleak. "But I can't sacrifice my family's future either."

From the beginning Lark had dreaded this moment and now she knew she'd been right to worry. She wasn't romantic and passionate like Skye, who'd willingly turned her back on her family and entrusted her whole world to the man she loved. "Then you must do what you believe is right." Her whole body went cold. "And so must I."

She backed away and fled to the nursery, confident he wouldn't follow. Sensing her distress, Nicki had stuck to her like glue. The closed door and white noise player that helped Grace sleep drowned any sound of the front door opening and closing. Lark sat in the room's rocking chair and absently stroked Nicki's head until she'd recovered enough to process the last ten minutes.

Did she really believe that Keaton had used her? She rubbed her temples. Surely if he wanted a partner for sex, he could snap his fingers and have a dozen gorgeous women flock to him. He might have been oblivious of the stir he'd created among several of the women at the Richardsons' party, but she hadn't. But with her mother's vile suspicions bolstering a lifetime of social awkwardness, Lark had fallen into a familiar mind-set.

But love? That seemed too far-fetched. Nor had he looked particularly happy to admit it. He'd chosen his family over her. The same way she'd chosen hers over him. They weren't at all like Jake and Skye. Those two had given up everything they'd ever known to be together. Neither Keaton nor Lark was willing to make that sort of sacrifice. That proved, however much they cared about each other, it wasn't truly love.

Calmer by the moment, Lark at last felt strong enough to stop reacting and move forward. She called her friend Julie and asked if she could watch Grace for a couple hours. Her parents needed to know what Keaton had found. It was important that they knew what was coming.

An hour later, she turned her car onto the long

driveway that led to the Taylor ranch house. Leaving Nicki in the car, she approached the house. It wasn't until she set her hand on the doorknob that she realized she'd been so consumed about talking to her parents that it hadn't occurred to her to call and make sure they were home. To her relief, her father was in his favorite chair in the great room.

"Lark, what brings you here?" Her father set aside the file he'd been reading and gestured her into a nearby chair. "You're upset. Nothing is wrong with Skye, is it?"

She'd called her parents yesterday with the news that Skye had awakened from her coma, and to her relief they'd rushed to the hospital. For a little while they'd been a family once again, maybe not a particularly happy one, but at least for the duration of the visit, their focus had been on Skye.

"No, nothing like that," she assured him, sitting down on the edge of the chair. "It's about the land that borders the Holt property."

Tyrone's eyes narrowed to slits. "Let me guess, that Holt boy has convinced you the land belongs to his family."

Lark ignored the acid in his voice. "He found the bill of sale at the town hall that predates the one that entitles us to that land."

"Oh, he just found it." Her father eyed her in disgust. "You were always book smart and not very good with people."

She couldn't deny her lack of social skills, but she'd seen no evidence that any of the Holts lied or cheated. They'd been nothing but kind to her and considerate of Skye and Grace. Lark's head spun. Or was that what she wanted to believe because she'd fallen in love with Keaton?

"Can't you at least sit down and talk with Keaton? It would save both sides a huge legal battle."

"A legal battle we are going to win."

Although she'd known this would be her father's answer, disappointment swept over Lark. In the back of her mind, she'd held on to the tiniest bit of hope that her father would be reasonable for once in his life.

"You don't know that. What if the land isn't ours? You're going to waste money and time fighting a losing battle."

"It's Taylor land."

His vehemence threw Lark back into her childhood. For a moment she wasn't a twenty-seven-year-old woman, but a girl of eight watching from the front seat of a pickup as her father drove his fist into David Holt's jaw. The blow had been followed up by another to his opponent's stomach. It wasn't the fight that had frightened her, but her father's savage delight. It had taken three men to restrain him.

Suddenly Lark had heard enough. "I'm sick of this stupid feud," she cried, pushing to her feet. "It's a couple thousand acres of land. Fighting over it has done nothing but hurt people. It drove Skye away. She left because she fell in love with Jake and no one could accept it."

"She didn't run away," Tyrone said. "When I found out she'd been sleeping with that Holt boy, I threw her out."

"What?" All this time Lark believed her parents had given Skye an ultimatum and that she'd chosen Jake. "She was your favorite. You loved her."

"She betrayed us." Her father rose.

Lark couldn't believe what she was hearing. "She didn't betray you." Again her thoughts turned to Skye and what she must have gone through in those days after her relationship with Jake had been discovered. Lark would give anything to take back her unsupportive behavior and longed to ask her sister how she'd coped. "She fell in love."

"Is that what you did? Your mother tells me you're sleeping with the elder Holt boy."

The change of topic caught Lark off guard. She should have come prepared to defend herself, but her emotions were too raw for clear thinking. "He's not using me, if that's what you think."

"What I think is you didn't have much experience with boys in high school. I'm guessing that continued in college. The Holts are liars and cheats. You should have known better than to let him trick you."

"I haven't." But wasn't that what she'd accused him of doing? Before she'd had dealings with them, Lark had always assumed there was something shifty about the Holts. She'd trusted her father's judgment, but now that she'd gotten to know Keaton and his parents, she had a different perspective.

Her father turned fierce blue eyes on her. "He created a fake document that he's going to use to cheat us out of our land."

"Keaton wouldn't do that."

"Sure he would. He's a Holt, isn't he?"

"That's ridiculous. Keaton is honest and honorable. He would never do something so underhanded."

Where had this reasonableness been an hour ago when she was throwing accusations at Keaton? Maybe if she'd taken a moment to think it all through she wouldn't have treated him so unfairly. Would he ever be able to forgive her?

"You are no different than your sister, siding with them against your own family."

"I'm not siding with anyone against you, but if he's had the document authenticated, surely that means something went wrong a hundred years ago."

"That's impossible. It was lost years ago."

"Lost?" At first Lark was too shocked to understand; then as her father's meaning penetrated, she gasped. "The Holts have always claimed there was a bill of sale. You've always claimed there was no such document. Now you say it was lost. Which is it?"

Her father glared at her, but uncertainty flickered for a moment in his gaze. "The land is ours."

"But did the Holts buy the land first?"

"There might have been a sale, but there was no official record."

"Because proof of the sale wasn't recorded." Appalled, Lark saw that her father wasn't as certain of his position as he'd been moments before. Her heart softened. Had he taken his aggressive stance against the Holts all these years because of fear? "The land does belong to the Holts."

Any doubt she'd glimpsed in her father vanished at her words. He stalked to the door and opened it. "Get out of my house and don't bother coming back until you change your tune."

While father and daughter stared at each other, a large figure filled the open doorway.

"Lark?" It was Keaton. He gazed from her to her father, assessing the situation. "Is everything okay here?" He hadn't entered the Taylor home, but looked prepared to do so on Lark's word.

Her heart floundered in her chest. What was he doing here? The concern in his gaze sent regret and shame rushing through her. She'd been so wrong to accuse him of using her. She'd let fear and old prejudices guide her to make terrible assumptions.

"I came to tell my father about the bill of sale you found." She began to edge toward the door, toward Keaton, giving her father a wide berth. "I asked him to sit down and discuss the situation rather than getting the courts involved."

Keaton looked surprised. She tried to convey her apology without words, but he'd switched his attention to her father. "Tyrone." Keaton pitched his voice in polite and moderate tones. "I want to work out something with the land that will benefit both our families."

"It's not your land."

"I have a bill of sale that says it is."

"It's a fake."

Lark could see her father's conviction had flagged. Yet he was a stubborn, single-minded man who'd been fighting a battle against the Holts all his life.

He'd never admit that what he knew as truth might be wrong.

"Father, please listen to what Keaton has to say." As she spoke, she moved to stand beside Keaton. His solid strength comforted her, enabled her to feel safe for the first time since she'd entered her father's home. "He's fair and honest. You can trust him."

Tyrone's upper lip curled in derision. "So you've chosen. Very well. From here on out, you are no more my daughter than that sister of yours."

"Father!" Lark took an involuntary step backward. The movement put her outside the house on the wide front porch. She bumped into Keaton and felt him grip her upper arms, steadying her. "You don't mean that."

"I do indeed. You've placed your loyalty with the Holts. I am finished with you."

Her father closed the door with an emphatic finality, underscored by the sound of a dead bolt being thrown.

Conscious of Keaton's worried expression, Lark descended the porch steps. Her emotions whirled and dipped like a carnival ride. She'd just been tossed out of the family. Had her father lost his mind? Was two thousand acres of land worth more than her and Skye?

"Lark, I'm so sorry," Keaton said, catching her

arm and turning her to face him. "I never meant for any of that to happen."

Of course he hadn't. That was the sort of man he was. He'd suggested working with her father to give him a lease on water rights from the disputed property. Lark knew her father would never have made a similar offer to Keaton.

"It's okay." She raised her hand and put it on his chest.

He immediately covered her hand with his. "No, it's not. Your father just disowned you."

"Really...?"

To Lark's amazement she felt lighter, less encumbered, than she'd ever known. Was this what Skye had felt when she left town with Jake? Had she felt free to do and be whatever she wanted without the weight of their parents' expectations and disapproval dragging her down?

Lark sucked in a huge breath, and the fresh air infused her with glee. At last she was free to love the man standing before her without agonizing over what would happen when her parents found out and how angry they'd be. She was her own person. The only person she had to worry about disappointing was herself. And she would be terribly unhappy with herself if she pushed Keaton away again.

"It's okay." She beamed at him. "I'm okay."

* * *

Unsure if Lark was suffering from hysteria or shock, Keaton scrutinized her closely. "I don't understand. Aren't you upset?"

"I might be later, but for now all I feel is relief."

When he'd left her house he went straight to his parents and told them about the bill of sale and Lark's reaction to the news of its reappearance. He'd been certain that he'd lost her and determined to do whatever he could to win her back. He'd offer to split the land. Even compensate the Taylors for their loss. But he couldn't do any of that without his parents' approval.

He'd never expected to turn up at the Taylor Ranch in time to hear her side with him against her father. She'd chosen him over her family.

"Relief?" he asked. "Why?"

To his delight, she lifted up on tiptoe and wrapped her arms around his neck. "Because I love you and I don't care who knows it." She planted a hard kiss on his lips and pulled back to grin at him, her smile one of wild, unfettered joy.

His arms went around her and pulled her tight. She loved him. Hearing her say those words made him happier than he'd ever been. "You chose me over your parents."

"I was stupid not to do so a long time ago. You

are the most caring, intelligent, sexiest man on the planet, and until today I hadn't fully appreciated how lost I would be without you."

"I'm glad to hear you say that, because this afternoon I was terrified I'd lost you. In fact, after our fight, I realized what needed to happen and went back to the house looking for you. Julie told me you were here and I came to lend you my support."

"Of course you did." Her eyes were bright and trusting. "Thank you."

"Let's get out of here," Keaton suggested, all too aware that her father could be loading a shotgun at this very moment with the idea of running him off Taylor land. "I have something I want to talk to you about. Follow me in your car."

She looked puzzled by his request but nodded. Halfway down the Taylors' driveway, around a curve and out of sight of the house, Keaton turned onto a little-used track that wound past the tree farm and entered the land that had been in dispute for so many generations. He was sure Lark had an idea where he was heading, and when he at last stopped the truck and got out to meet her, he could see she was smiling.

"The swimming hole I used to come to in the summer," she said, her eyebrows raised. "Where you used to spy on me."

Keaton took her hand and led her down the path to the water's edge, the Aussie frolicking around them. "I was old enough to know better," he admitted, watching Nicki chase a rabbit that was darting for cover. "But I couldn't bring myself to stop. It was the only time I'd ever seen you truly happy." He cast a sideways glance in her direction. "And then there was how you looked in that bikini."

"It was one of Skye's old ones. We weren't exactly the same size, so it didn't fit all that well."

In fact, it had been incredibly indecent on her lush curves. And she hadn't cared in the least. Keaton had loved every second she'd spent near or in the water. Her laughter had been infectious. Her sexy strut along the beach, laughably awkward and all the more delicious for its unconventional style, had sent his hormones into a tailspin.

"You were gorgeous in it." His voice had lowered into a husky murmur. "Any chance it's languishing in a drawer somewhere?"

Lark laughed. "Not likely."

"Pity." He pulled her along the edge of the water. The ten-acre lake wasn't the largest on the property, and the Taylors didn't use it to irrigate the tree farm. But it sat exactly in the middle of the two thousand acres that had been in dispute. "But I didn't bring you here to reminisce," he explained, looping his arm around her. "I've decided this land needs to be claimed by both our families, so I intend to build a house here."

She surveyed the lake. "It'll be a fantastic spot. But won't that mean the ranch house will be empty a lot of the time now that your parents have bought property in Alabama?"

"I think a married man ought to have his own house, don't you?"

"Sure." She drew the word out. "Your wife would want the freedom to decorate and run her own household." She peered at him from beneath her lashes, her expression leaning toward somber. "And it's about time you thought about settling down. You're not getting any younger."

"You sound like my mother," he groused, but a smile lurked in his tone.

"But you said the land should be claimed by both our families, so what else did you have in mind? Some sort of compound where I live on the opposite side of the lake? And maybe Jake and Skye would consider a vacation home here."

"I'm not really sure that would work for me," Keaton said, pulling her close. "You'd be a little too far away for my taste."

Her eyes widened with pleasure. "You want to live together?"

"That's been working out pretty well this last month."

Her brow furrowed as she considered his proposition. "I've really enjoyed spending time with you, so I say let's do it."

"You've enjoyed spending time with me?" he echoed. "Ten minutes ago you claimed you loved me."

"Well, yes. I do."

"And you may recall that I told you at your house that I had fallen in love with you, as well."

"You meant that?"

"Of course I did. Do you think I run around telling women that I'm in love with them when I'm not?"

"Have you been in love with a lot of women?"

Keaton snorted. "Only you. Which is why..." He reached into his pocket and pulled out a small burgundy box. "Lark Marie Taylor." He popped the top on the box and watched her eyes widen at its contents. "Will you marry me? I want to build our dream house on this spot and live happily ever after with you."

Her eyes glowed like twin emeralds as she answered, "Absolutely."

He slipped the ring from the box and onto her trembling finger. As they sealed their pledge with a long, deep kiss, the rest of the world faded. Much, much later he felt the cool breeze against his hot skin and realized they'd been lost in each other for a quite a while.

"We should probably continue this at home," he said, setting his forehead against hers. "I'm sure Julie wasn't expecting you to be gone this long and may be worried."

"I sent her a quick text before getting out of the car and let her know we'd been delayed."

And that was one of the things he loved about Lark. Always considering others and acting with efficiency. Opposites might attract, but what had drawn Keaton to Lark was all the ways she understood and accepted him.

"You know what this means," Lark said, laughing with joy. "We've officially ended the Holt/Taylor feud. After us there will be no more generations of your family and my family. It will all be our family."

"I think that sounds pretty great," he said. "And speaking of our family, how eager are you to start one?"

"Very," she admitted. "Having Grace around this last month has made me anxious for children of my own. How do you feel?"

"The same."

Her smile grew wicked. "Then what are we doing standing around here?"

Chuckling, he drew Lark back to where they'd left their vehicles. The afternoon sun was fading toward the horizon, painting the lake and surrounding trees with a golden light. He gave the scene a final look as he opened Lark's car door, picturing a big house by this lake with children running in the yard. It was going to be a perfect place to build a life with her. He imagined their sons and daughters growing up on the land that had kept their families at odds for decades, their happiness banishing old resentment.

"What do you see?" she asked, noticing his distraction.

"Our future." He brushed his lips against hers. "And it looks absolutely wonderful."

* * * * *